You're About to Become a
Privileged Woman.

INTRODUCING
PAGES & PRIVILEGES™.

It's our way of thanking you for buying
our books at your favorite retail store.

GET ALL THIS FREE
WITH JUST ONE PROOF OF PURCHASE:

◆ **Hotel Discounts** up
to 60% at home and
abroad ◆ **Travel Service**
- Guaranteed lowest
published airfares
plus 5% cash back

$50 VALUE

on tickets ◆ **$25 Travel Voucher**
◆ **Sensuous Petite Parfumerie** collection

◆ **Insider Tips Letter**
with sneak previews
of upcoming books

You'll get ... ...
It's your p... ...nd to
even mo... ...ne!
There's no club to ... ... obligation.

Enrollment Form

☐ *Yes!* I WANT TO BE A *P*RIVILEGED *W*OMAN.

Enclosed is one *PAGES & PRIVILEGES*™ Proof of Purchase from any Harlequin or Silhouette book currently for sale in stores (Proofs of Purchase are found on the back pages of books) and the store cash register receipt. Please enroll me in *PAGES & PRIVILEGES*™. Send my Welcome Kit and FREE Gifts -- and activate my FREE benefits -- immediately.

More great gifts and benefits to come like these luxurious Truly Lace and L'Effleur gift baskets.

▶ DETACH HERE AND MAIL TODAY! ▶

NAME (please print)
_____

ADDRESS _____ APT. NO _____

CITY _____ STATE _____ ZIP/POSTAL CODE _____

PROOF OF PURCHASE
SAMPLE ONLY

Please allow 6-8 weeks for delivery. Quantities are limited. We reserve the right to substitute items. Enroll before October 31, 1995 and receive one full year of benefits.

NO CLUB!
NO COMMITMENT!
Just one purchase brings you great Free Gifts and Benefits!
(More details in back of this book.)

Name of store where this book was purchased_____

Date of purchase_____

Type of store:

☐ Bookstore   ☐ Supermarket   ☐ Drugstore

☐ Dept. or discount store (e.g. K-Mart or Walmart)

☐ Other (specify)_____

Pages & Privileges™

Which Harlequin or Silhouette series do you usually read?
_____

Complete and mail with one Proof of Purchase and store receipt to:

U.S.: *PAGES & PRIVILEGES*™, P.O. Box 1960, Danbury, CT 06813-1960

Canada: *PAGES & PRIVILEGES*™, 49-6A The Donway West, P.O. 813, North York, ON M3C 2E8   **PRINTED IN U.S.A**

"I'm so grateful to you, Ramón…" Tanya said.

"When you kissed me, then, was it out of gratitude?" he asked softly.

"I don't know," she answered. "I don't think so."

"I don't think so, either." With a suddenness that surprised her, he bent and pressed another kiss to her mouth. The kiss carried a strong edge of hunger.

"It wasn't gratitude, Tanya. We were attracted to each other years ago, and we still are. It isn't wrong, and it doesn't have to go anywhere."

She looked at him. "I don't know how to do that… be lighthearted about kissing you, about feeling attracted to you."

Ramón's devastating smile showed off his white teeth and made his eyes crinkle at the corners. He winked. "Stick with me, kid."

Tanya just smiled. She doubted anyone could teach her to laugh again—but if anyone could, it was Ramón….

Dear Reader,

Special Edition's lineup for August will definitely make this a memorable summer of romance! Our THAT SPECIAL WOMAN! title for this month is *The Bride Price* by reader favorite Ginna Gray. Wyatt Sommersby has his work cut out for him when he tries to convince the freedom-loving Maggie Muldoon to accept his proposal of marriage.

Concluding the new trilogy MAN, WOMAN AND CHILD this month is *Nobody's Child* by Pat Warren. Don't miss the final installment of this innovative series. Also in August, we have three veteran authors bringing you three wonderful new stories. In *Scarlet Woman* by Barbara Faith, reunited lovers face their past and once again surrender to their passion. *What She Did on Her Summer Vacation* is Tracy Sinclair's story of a young woman on holiday who finds herself an instant nanny to two adorable kids—and the object of a young aristocrat's affections. Ruth Wind's *The Last Chance Ranch* is the emotional story of one woman's second chance at life when she reclaims her child. Finally, August introduces *New York Times* bestseller Ellen Tanner Marsh to Silhouette Special Edition. She brings her popular and unique style to her first story for us, *A Family of Her Own*. This passionate and heartwarming tale is one you won't want to miss.

This summer of love and romance isn't over yet! I hope you enjoy each and every story to come!

Sincerely,

Tara Gavin, Senior Editor

Please address questions and book requests to:
Silhouette Reader Service
U.S.: 3010 Walden Ave., P.O. Box 1325, Buffalo, NY 14269
Canadian: P.O. Box 609, Fort Erie, Ont. L2A 5X3

RUTH
WIND
THE LAST CHANCE RANCH

Published by Silhouette Books
America's Publisher of Contemporary Romance

This is for the friend of my heart,
Sharon Lynn High Williams, a tireless warrior for the lost children; a lamp in the darkness, burning bright.
With love and admiration.

 SILHOUETTE BOOKS

ISBN 0-373-09977-0

THE LAST CHANCE RANCH

Copyright © 1995 by Barbara Samuel

This edition published by arrangement with Harlequin Books S.A.

® and TM are trademarks of Harlequin Books S.A., used under license. Trademarks indicated with ® are registered in the United States Patent and Trademark Office, the Canadian Trade Marks Office and in other countries.

Printed in U.S.A.

Books by Ruth Wind

Silhouette Special Edition

Strangers on a Train #555
Summer's Freedom #588
Light of Day #635
A Minute To Smile #742
Jezebel's Blues #785
Walk In Beauty #881
The Last Chance Ranch #977

Silhouette Intimate Moments

Breaking the Rules #587

RUTH WIND

is the award-winning author of both contemporary and historical romance novels. She lives in the mountainous Southwest with her husband, two growing sons and many animals in a hundred-year-old house the town blacksmith built. The only hobby she has since she started writing is tending the ancient garden of irises, lilies and lavender beyond her office window, and she says she can think of no more satisfying way to spend a life than growing children, books and flowers.

COLORADO

Last Chance Ranch

Manzanares

Sangre de Cristo Mountains

Santa Fe

Albuquerque

ARIZONA

TEXAS

Rio Grande

NEW MEXICO

N

MEXICO

All underlined places are fictitious.

Prologue

On her twenty-second birthday, Tanya Bishop took her three-year-old son Antonio to see a Disney movie. They returned home late, and Antonio was asleep on her shoulder when she unlocked the door.

She knew Victor had found her again the minute she stepped into the house. Something just didn't feel right.

Halting on the threshold with Antonio asleep in her arms, Tanya listened to the darkness. Her instincts prickled. From the kitchen came the predictable plop of water from the leaky faucet, and the warm hum of the refrigerator. Though she waited a full minute, holding her breath, she heard nothing else.

Cautiously, she eased in far enough to flip on the lights in the living room. The lamp on the coffee table burst alive and illuminated a room that looked exactly as it had when she left. A little cluttered but basically clean.

Still she held the slack body of her son against her and waited, listening for another moment. Nothing.

Tanya walked to the kitchen, inky dark at the end of the hall. Her footsteps made the old floor creak. In her arms, Antonio stirred and lifted his head, then settled it again on her shoulder. She could feel his hot, moist breath on her neck.

In the kitchen, she lost her nerve to be still and quiet, and flipped on the light in a rush. The fluorescent tubing spluttered as it always did, the gases heating slowly, dimly, then flaring to abrupt life.

On the floor, in shattered, tiny pieces, was Tanya's china. The exquisite saucers and one-of-a-kind dinner plates that she had collected for years were shattered all over the kitchen. He'd ground some below his boots, for the china was powdered in places, and the linoleum below it gouged with the ferocity of Victor's rage.

Tanya stared at the leavings of his violence and fought back tears. She had a restraining order against him, but he ignored it. Seven times she'd called the police and signed complaints. In desperation, she had gone into hiding, moving every three months so he would never know for sure where she was. He tracked her each time, once all the way to Santa Fe.

A deep and painful ache of fear beat in her chest. This time, he would kill her. Two days ago, he'd accosted her at a supermarket, in front of witnesses, and the police had arrested him. Now he was out of jail, and he knew where to find her.

Very slowly, she backed out of the kitchen.

It all counted against her later.

Tanya settled Tonio on the couch and filled his day care bag with extra clothes, his teddy bear and the blanket he could not sleep without, plenty of underwear and his favorite toys. Then she sat down in her kitchen, brushing shards of china from the table and chair, and wrote her son a letter which she tucked in among his things.

She took him to a day care home she trusted, then drove back to her house. It was just past eleven.

In the ruins of her kitchen, she sat down to wait.

And as she waited, she remembered... Victor, winking at her across the crowded school auditorium the first time she'd seen him. The gentle trembling of his hands as he kissed her the first time. The passionate avowals of love he'd pressed upon her. The flowers he brought in apology when his temper had got the better of him. The jealous rages that had become more and more frequent. ...

At 2:37, she heard Victor at the back door, drunk and cursing as he jimmied the lock. She lifted the phone and dialed 911.

Victor kicked the door. "I'm gonna kill you, Annie!" He kicked it again and the windows rattled under the impact.

To the girl at the end of the emergency line, Tanya said, "I need the police at 132 Mariposa. A man is breaking into my house." She knew if she said it was her ex-husband the police wouldn't come as quickly.

Victor roared an obscenity and kicked the door. Tanya winced. "Please hurry," she begged and dropped the phone. She ran for her bedroom, hearing the threshold splinter as Victor barreled into the back room. He roared his name for her. Tanya scrambled in her drawer for the loaded revolver she'd put there, and rushed into the bathroom.

In the bathroom, she locked the door and crouched in a corner, praying in the nonsensical words of the terrified, "Please, please, please." The words meant *please make him go away* and *please don't let him find me* and *please don't let him hurt me anymore*. Last time, oh, last time—

"Annie!" In the living room, she heard things breaking, and chairs being overturned, and a low growling roar that struck a panting, mindless terror through her. He didn't even know he did it. But that animal sound meant his temper was beyond all mortal limits, that drink and rage had turned him into a beast.

A beast that had mauled her in the past.

Not again. She clasped the gun between her violently trembling, sweaty hands. In the distance, she heard sirens.

Please, please, please.

"Annie!" Something else was turned over.

He kicked or hit the bathroom door and Tanya couldn't halt the sob of terror that escaped her lips. She closed her eyes as he began to batter the door, lifted the gun as he yelled her name again. Tears came. Tears for everything—so many good things and so many bad—ran in great washes down her cheeks. She had to use a wrist to wipe them away.

The sirens came closer. The door gave with a splintering sound. Victor, savage as a rabid bear, tumbled into the room.

Not again! her heart cried. *Not again.*

Sobbing, Tanya aimed the gun at his chest and pulled the trigger.

It was the last thing she remembered.

Chapter One

Dear Antonio,
They called him a hanging judge. Everybody says it might have gone better if I'd had the money for a real good lawyer, but I didn't, so I'm going to spend a long time behind bars.

Maybe it would be okay, if I could see you sometimes, but your dad's sisters want you protected. From me, I guess. And someone has to take care of you while I'm in here. If I do what they want, then I can pick who takes care of you. It won't be one of them.

So I signed the papers they brought to me, giving custody to your dad's cousin, Ramón

Quezada. He's a fine man, and very smart. He'll take good care of you.

Be good.

Love, Mom

Eleven years later

As the bus pulled into the dun-colored adobe bus station at Manzanares, New Mexico, Tanya Bishop scanned the concrete apron for the man who was supposed to be meeting her. She remembered Ramón Quezada from a wedding reception fifteen years ago. She had danced with him. He'd been skinny then, an intense and bespectacled college student. His probing intelligence had intrigued and thrilled her even as it made her uncomfortably aware of all she wanted to understand and didn't.

Her most vivid memory of Ramón, however, was the tape that had held his glasses together after Victor hit him for dancing with her.

Peering through the bus windows, Tanya saw no one who even remotely fit her memories. She clutched her purse more tightly in her fingers, feeling the leather grow slick against her palms. What if he'd forgotten he was supposed to meet her?

No. Ridiculous. She took a steadying breath. He would not forget. Ramón was responsible, trustworthy, honest and loyal—all the things his cousin Victor had not been.

All the things Antonio needed.

As the brakes on the lumbering bus whooshed to a stop, Tanya saw a man come through the glass doors that led to the inner terminal. He was dressed all in black—black jeans, black cotton cowboy shirt with pearlescent snaps, black jean jacket lined with sheepskin. Her stomach flipped. He sort of looked like Ramón. But that couldn't be the skinny man-child she remembered.

Could it?

He was the right height—Ramón had been rather tall. He was the right age—about middle thirties now. But that lean, dangerous creature could not possibly be the same man she'd danced with so long ago. She leaned forward, frowning in disbelief.

It was him. Ramón Quezada, her late husband's cousin, the fearless leader of the Last Chance Ranch, and her son Antonio's adoptive father.

He bore the distinctive Quezada family stamp, a long-limbed grace that spoke of centuries of working with horses; hair so black it seemed to gleam with internal light; even the arrogant nose, so beautifully formed, high-bridged and straight. A conquistador's nose, Tanya thought. And the high cheekbones were Apache. A hard lot, the Quezadas. Fighting men.

Time had done good things to him. Tanya clutched her bag to the sudden ache in her chest. Ramón's long wavy hair curled in an unruly way around his neck, inviting female fingers to smooth it. He moved with the calm ease of a man at home with himself and his world. Tanya saw a woman pause at the doors and take a second look over her shoulder at him.

Passengers filed down the aisle beside her, but Tanya found herself frozen in her seat, her gaze riveted to the spot where he waited, his intense gaze fixed on the disembarking passengers. She had briefed herself on everything from the right clothes to bring to a ranch for troubled boys, to brushing up on her colloquial Spanish, to the enormous task of girding herself to see her son again after eleven years. She had even braced herself to hide her identity from that son, in order to allow a relationship to develop naturally between them.

She had not prepared herself to deal with a man who wore an aura of sex appeal like a second skin.

Had he always looked like this and she'd just been too much in love with Victor to notice? A pair of glasses might have hidden the stoked passion in his eyes, or covered the clean beauty of his bone structure, but nothing could have concealed a mouth so richly formed, so dangerously seductive.

Staring at him from the greatly mature age of thirty-three, Tanya thought—not for the first time— that she had been one of the most foolish young girls ever to inhabit the planet.

Another woman might have sighed in pleasure at the prospect of living in close quarters with such a man for the next few months. Another woman might have allowed the dark wash of desire to flow through her in anticipation of kindling the banked passion in that face. Another woman might have let her gaze wander over that lean, long-limbed body and wondered how it would feel against her own.

Tanya did not have the luxury.

For one long moment of panic, she considered just staying on the bus, letting it carry her to the next stop. From there, she'd call the ranch and tell Ramón she'd changed her mind.

On the platform, he glanced around with a frown, and Tanya knew she couldn't walk away. He'd done a lot for her, even more for her son Antonio.

And if she didn't get off the bus now, her chances of ever seeing her son again were next to nothing.

Clutching her bag to her chest, Tanya stood up. Around her, the last passengers murmured in a musical mingling of Spanish and English. She took in a long breath and squared her shoulders, then marched down the aisle.

Outside on the platform, Tanya lost sight of Ramón. People surged around her—grandmothers gathering children, sweethearts hugging each other—and Tanya was struck unexpectedly with a sharp arrow of joy. She was free! Not as she had been at the halfway house, but truly and honestly free. Free to smell diesel fuel and hear ordinary swearing, free to touch people and be bumped. Through the garage door, she caught a glimpse of dark clouds rolling in from the west, and it occurred to her that she was free to stand in the rain if she chose. For as long as she wanted to...

A male voice sounded at her elbow, "Annie?"

The pet name was uttered in a voice almost too familiar—slightly accented and beautifully sonorous. A bolt of terror replaced her joy, and she squeezed her eyes tight. It was just a nightmare, she told herself, a nightmare like all the others she had suffered the past eleven years, dreams of Victor coming after her again. Cold sweat broke out on her body.

The man at her side touched her arm, as if to steady her, and Tanya yanked away violently, nearly stumbling in her haste to get away.

Reason belatedly waded into her terror. It wasn't Victor, because Victor was dead. Tanya halted, then turned very slowly.

Ramón stood there, even more overwhelmingly attractive at close range. He kept his distance a little warily, his hands lifted, palms out, to show her he wouldn't hurt her. She was sure he was wondering what kind of basket case he'd saddled himself with.

"Please don't call me Annie," she said in a tone as even as she could muster. "It was Victor's name for me. No one else ever called me that."

"I'm sorry." There was genuine regret in his voice. "I didn't mean to startle you." Ramón reached for the duffel bag that contained all her earthly goods. "Let's put this in the truck, all right?"

Mutely, Tanya followed him into the dark autumn day. A sharp wind blew from the Sangre de Cristos Mountains, slicing viciously through her thin cloth coat. With a small shiver, she clutched it closer to her body, bending her head into the burst of bitter wind.

Ramón caught the movement. "Not much of a coat for this kind of weather." Reaching into the cab, he brought forth a down parka and held it out to her. "It's a nasty day, but Indian summer will be back tomorrow."

Tanya was unaccustomed to simple kindness, and for a minute, she hesitated. A gust of wind blasted them, tossing hair over Ramón's solemn face. With a dark, long-fingered hand, he brushed it away.

"Thank you," she said. Shyly, she traded coats, giving him the old one, which he tossed into the truck.

Buttoning his own jacket, he asked, "What would you like for lunch—American or Mexican? The Blue Swan has great green chili, and Yolanda's has good fried chicken."

Tanya shrugged. "I don't care."

"Me, either," he said. "You choose."

She didn't want to choose. She'd used up all her reserves of emotional energy, and there was still Antonio to think about. For herself, she'd like the green chili, but maybe Ramón would like hamburgers. She said nothing.

Nor did he. The silence between them stretched to a strained, awkward length. Tanya stuffed her hands in her pockets and waited.

At last he prodded her. "What would you like—Tanya? Can I call you Tanya?"

"Tanya is fine." She took a breath and chose, watching his face carefully for subtle signs of disapproval. "I guess green chili sounds good."

He smiled. The expression transformed his face, giving a twinkle to the depthless eyes, adding emphasis to the high slant of cheekbones. Tanya's chest, tight with anxiety, eased with an abruptness that made her almost dizzy. She'd made the right choice.

Ramón stirred sugar into his coffee and watched Tanya carefully tear the wrapping from a straw. From the speakers in the ceiling came a soft Spanish ballad, mournful with strummed guitars and flutes. For a moment, he was transported to another day, another time, when he'd danced with this woman, when she had been a sweet, pretty young girl . . . and he'd fallen in love.

In those days, he'd often fallen in love. More often than not, his passion had gone unrequited. Upon meeting Tanya for the first time, so many years ago, he'd thought his infatuation was like all the others.

But in Tanya's beautiful dark blue eyes there had been an almost painful yearning for things unnameable and unattainable. It had struck him deeply. As he'd held her loosely, her blond hair spilling over her shoulders, her youthful eighteen-year-old body swelling just slightly with the baby in her tummy, she'd told him about a book she was reading, *Tortilla Flat*. She'd said the name as if it were new, as if no one had ever discovered it before, and there had been magic and wonder in her tone, in her sweet innocence.

That she had reached the age of eighteen without knowing such a work existed, that she could find it on her own and love it with such passion, had touched Ramón in some quiet place. Until that day, he'd been too enmeshed in his anger to see what was plain if only he looked around him—a person didn't have to be brown or black or red to suffer the indignities of ignorance and poverty. The realization that social class, not race, was the great deciding factor in American society had changed his life.

They had talked all afternoon, while Victor—Tanya's husband and Ramón's cousin—drank in the bar with the wedding party. They talked about books and movies, about ideas and hopes and plans. As he listened to her sweet, soft voice, and watched her eyes shine with excitement, Ramón had fallen in love.

And when Victor, drunk and evil-tempered, broke Ramón's cheekbone, Ramón had almost felt it was deserved. Tanya was Victor's wife, after all.

Ramón had gone back to Albuquerque, to his Latin-American studies, and had tried to wipe the beautiful young girl from his mind. He hadn't known until almost a year later that Tanya, too, had paid for that golden afternoon. Victor had beaten her senseless and she'd landed in the hospital with seven broken bones, including ribs and wrist. By some miracle, the baby had survived. Tanya briefly left her husband after the hospital had released her, but Victor promised to give up drinking. Tanya had returned to him, and Victor kept his promise.

For a little while, anyway.

Looking now at the woman the girl had become, Ramón felt a little dizzy with lost chances and lost hopes and ruined dreams. She was not the softly round girl he'd been smitten with that day so long ago. Her hair was not curled and wispy, but cut straight across so it hung like a gleaming golden brown curtain at her shoulders. Her face and body were thinner and harder, lean as a coyote's. She had a long, ropy kind of muscle in her upper arms, the kind that came from sustained hard work.

Her exotically beautiful blue eyes were wary as they met his. "Do I have something on my chin?" she asked.

He shook his head, smiling. "Sorry. I was just remembering the last time I saw you."

The faintest hint of a smile curved her pretty mouth. "Boy, that was forever ago. Another lifetime."

"It was." He took a breath, trying to think of a way to pick his way through the minefield of memories. He opted for flattery. "You were so pretty I couldn't believe you danced with me."

A small wash of rose touched her cheeks. She glanced out the window, then back to him. "What I remember is how smart you were. You talked to me like I was smart, too. It meant a lot to me."

Ramón smiled at her, feeling a warmth he'd thought far beyond his reach. "Me, too."

At that moment, the waitress brought their food. Ramón leaned back and let go of a breath as the waitress put his plate down. Things would be all right. He hadn't been sure.

Once she got some hot food inside her hollow stomach, Tanya felt stronger. The stamina and common strength she'd worked to build for eleven years seeped back, and with it, a sense of normalcy.

With a sigh, she leaned back in the turquoise vinyl booth. "Much better."

"Good."

The waitress came by with a steel coffeepot, topped their cups, and whisked away Tanya's empty bowl. "I'm sorry I seemed so strange back at the station," Tanya said. "It's just a little overwhelming."

"Don't apologize. I'm sorry I startled you." He finished the last bites of an enormous smothered burrito and pushed the plate to one side. "Let's start fresh."

"Okay." She attempted a smile, and felt the unused muscles in her face creak only a little. "Didn't you wear glasses?"

"Yeah." His grin was wry. "I'm blind as a bat, but glasses aren't real practical on a ranch." He touched his lips with his napkin. "Weren't you blonde?"

"Sort of," she said with a shrug. "Victor liked my hair light, so I dyed it for him. This is the natural color."

"I like it." His gaze lingered, and Tanya saw a shimmer of sexual approval in those unrelentingly black irises.

An answering spark lit somewhere deep and cold within her, and Tanya found herself noticing again his mouth—full-lipped and sensual. On another man, it would have seemed too lush, but amid the savagely beautiful planes and angles of his face, it seemed only to promise pleasure beyond all imagining.

The cinders of burned-out feelings within her flared a little brighter, stirring a soft, tiny flame of awareness she'd not known in a long, long time.

Abruptly she quenched it, stamping hard at the spark to kill it. She tore her gaze away and poked her soda with the straw. "Why don't you tell me about my job?"

As if he understood the reason for the abrupt change of subject, Ramón replied in an impersonal tone. "You'll be cooking. Desmary has needed someone for quite some time, but it's hard to find someone with institutional experience in such an underpopulated area."

Tanya couldn't resist a small, wry dig at her own background. "If it's institutional food you want, I'm a master."

He chuckled. "Good. Desmary, the head cook, can't move around as well as she used to, but there's no place else for her to go. You're going to be her feet and her helper." He paused to dip a chip in salsa. "She's pretty independent, so if you can be discreet about helping her, I'd appreciate it."

"No problem."

"We've got a full house at the moment, twenty-five boys. They all have KP, so basically you're in charge of just getting them fed, and they clean up. Anybody who wants to cook can sign up to help, and you'll usually have a couple of boys every day."

"How old are the kids?"

"The youngest right now is eight. They don't often get into serious trouble much earlier than that. The oldest is seventeen. Most of them are twelve to fifteen."

Tanya half smiled. "It's going to be quite a switch for me to go from an almost completely female environment to one dominated by males."

"And teenage boys are more male than they'll ever be again." Ramón shook his head. "There are few women out there. I'm trying to change that, so the boys can learn to treat women with respect." He lifted one shoulder. "You may not always get it."

"I can handle that."

"You'll have to."

That sounded a little intimidating. Tanya lifted her eyebrows in question.

"There are rules to create discipline and order, to teach the boys how to behave themselves. If one of them is disrespectful, you'll be expected to manage the situation.''

Tanya frowned. "What constitutes disrespectful?''

He grinned. "If it wouldn't have gone over in 1920, it won't go over now.''

"You're kidding.''

"Not at all.'' His face was sober, but the dark eyes shone with intense passion. "Some of these boys are like animals when they come to me. They don't know how to eat at the table, or how to dress for regular society. They treat women and girls like sluts or possessions, like a pair of shoes.''

Like a possession. Tanya felt the tightness in her chest again. That was the way Victor had treated her. And she'd allowed it for a long time. She looked away, to the calm scene beyond the windows.

"I'm trying to give them dignity, Tanya,'' he said. "I think you can help me.''

Dignity. What dignity had she had, all these years? Had she ever known it? "I'll do my best.''

"That's all I ask of anyone,'' he said, and picked up the check. "Are you ready?''

A swift wave of nerves and anticipation washed through her. "Yes.''

Chapter Two

Dear Antonio,

You must be starting kindergarten this year. I wish I could see you. I'd tell you to be sure to stand up straight and make sure your hands are clean before you go. If you want people to respect you, you have to hold your head high.

I've started school, too. I'll get my GED, then take some classes from the college instructors who volunteer out here. I'm not sure what I want to study, but it helps to pass the time, and I'm good at it. It's something I can use to hold my head up high.

Love, Mom

The ranch was twelve miles from town, over rutted gravel roads. Ramón, seeming to sense Tanya's sudden nervousness, kept up a steady narration as they drove. She was grateful.

He'd started the boy ranch seven years before, he told her. Using grants from several sources, he established it as a place for troubled young boys. From the beginning, his intention had been to provide an alternative to the usual reform schools and foster homes in which such children were normally placed.

"You'll forgive me for saying so, but I don't see how it can be much different."

He smiled. "Ah, but it is different. Everything is different."

"Like what?"

"Like I'm trying to give them an old-fashioned sense of belonging, a sense of family." He gave her a quick glance. "When I was working with these kids in Albuquerque, the thing I saw over and over was that there was no one to take care of them—give them meals on time, make sure they brushed their teeth and wore appropriate clothing. Until someone gave them that much dignity, a probation officer couldn't do much."

Tanya nodded slowly. "So who gets to live at the Last Chance?" The name made her smile.

"Only the worst ones."

"Doesn't that mean you lose a lot of them?"

His answer was unflinching and unsentimental. "Yes."

Tanya frowned. "Isn't that painful?"

He looked at her. "Every time." The muscle on his jaw drew tight and he cleared his throat. "We lost one last week when he went home on a weekend furlough. Tried to rob a convenience store and was shot while fleeing. Such a waste."

Tanya could tell by the roughness in his voice that he hadn't yet recovered from the loss. She wondered how he could stand to care so much, over and over again.

As if to gird himself, Ramón changed the subject. "They work hard, these kids. They plant and harvest our gardens, take care of the animals, clean the barns and rake the corrals. It makes them strong, gives them something to believe in."

"What kind of animals do you have?"

Ramón touched his chin, and Tanya picked up the faintest touch of embarrassment in the gesture. Puzzled, she waited for the answer.

"A lot of them," he said. "Goats, sheep, horses, cows, dogs, cats, rabbits, chickens. You name it, we've probably got it."

"Isn't it hard to feed all those animals?"

"Nah. We eventually butcher the chickens and rabbits, pigs and cows. Some of the boys don't like that duty, but most of them get around to appreciating the way food comes to the table after a while." He gave her a quick, amused glance. "Ever wrung a chicken's neck?"

Horrified, Tanya shook her head. "No!"

"Don't worry. Desmary will do it until you get used to the idea."

He said it as if she just naturally would get used to it. "All the food comes from the ranch?"

"As much as possible. It's part of teaching self-sufficiency." He turned onto a narrow dirt road and drove through a gate. "There's great dignity in providing for yourself."

"What about all the dogs and cats?"

He smiled. "Just for love. Nothing like a dog or a cat to love you when it seems like the whole world is against you."

Tanya looked at him. Against the cloudy sky, his profile was sharp, his expression certain and strong. "How did you make it happen?" she asked.

He glanced at her, then back to the road. On a rise, the buildings of the ranch appeared—a huge barn, a white farmhouse sitting in a copse of cottonwoods, three long wooden buildings with porches. "I worked with the probation system for six years, then my grandfather left me this land." He shrugged. "It seemed like it might be good for those boys to be closer to the land, so I wrote the proposals and got a bunch of grants."

He made it sound simple, but Tanya had a feeling the path had been far from easy.

They drew closer to the buildings, and anxiety sharp as talons clawed at Tanya. She could see figures moving in the corrals and around the house. Was

Antonio among them? "I'm so scared," she blurted out. "Do you think he'll recognize me?"

"No," he replied quietly. "He was only three, Tanya."

"I just don't want him to feel he has to like me or forgive me. I just want to see him." She swallowed. "So much."

"I know." He slowed a little, as if to give her time to collect herself. "This is best, his not knowing who you are right away. He doesn't understand the court orders, so he thinks you didn't want him."

A bitterness twisted her lips. She had been vulnerable after the trial, too weary to fight Victor's family any longer, and desperate to see that Antonio had a good home with someone she trusted. To make sure it was Ramón and not one of Victor's sisters, who hated her, Tanya had agreed to sever contact with Antonio as long as she was in jail. With her lawyer's help, she had managed to have the restriction lifted upon her release from prison, but that didn't make up for the lost eleven years. If she were Antonio, she'd feel betrayed, too.

She lifted her chin, feeling suddenly stronger. This was what she had waited for—to see her son again. Whether he knew she was his mother or not was beside the point. Thanks to Ramón's kindness, she would have the chance to know her child.

"Thank you, Ramón," she said. "You didn't have to give me this chance, and I am very grateful."

"De nada." He gave her a lazy wink. "I needed a cook."

Then they were pulling into the driveway, beneath the gold leaves on the branches of the cottonwood trees. A swarm of boys lifted their heads to watch. Tanya gathered her purse and put her hand on the door, scanning the faces eagerly. Would she even know him after so long?

Her gaze caught on a youth on the porch, eating an apple. Unlike Ramón, he wore his straight black hair short, combed back from his high forehead. The style showed off a dramatically carved and beautiful face—those heavy dark eyebrows, the distinctive and beautiful Quezada nose, his father's high cheek-bones—and Tanya's blue eyes, striking in the dark face.

She had been afraid she might cry, that even all those years of training herself to hide her emotions couldn't help her at this moment. Instead, as she stared at the face of her son after more than four thousand days of waiting, she smiled.

Ramón watched Tanya step out of the truck. There was shyness in the angle of her head, a certain hesitancy as she glanced at the pack of boys who milled toward her, but she didn't cower. He pursed his lips, watching them take her measure, and was pleased when her chin lifted, when she met their eyes without flinching.

Good, he thought. After the way she had reacted to him in the bus station, he had been afraid she wouldn't be able to stand up to this inspection, that her abusive relationship had ruined her permanently.

Standing there, her expression carefully neutral, she met the gaze of these rough boys with a roughness of her own. She knew where they came from. She'd been there. They saw it, too, and their predatory instincts were appeased, at least for the moment.

Ramón smiled. "Gentlemen," he said, in spite of the covert glances some of them swept over Tanya's shapely form, "this is our new cook, Ms. Bishop."

There were murmurs and nods. The newer boys looked to the ones who'd been residents longer for clues to the right behavior. "You'll meet everyone sooner or later," Ramón said, rounding the truck to stand near her. He pointed out and named a few of the closest faces, knowing the only one she would remember was the last. "The one on the porch is Tonio Quezada, my son."

Tanya nodded at all of them, smiling at the younger ones. Ramón was impressed when she managed the same polite nod toward her son as she had toward the others.

Then she looked up at Ramón with a smile of singular sweetness. Joy spilled from the wide blue eyes, eyes that somehow still carried a touching innocence. High color lit her cheeks. Her expression was meant to convey to him what she could not say in front of all these witnesses—the most heartfelt gratitude he'd ever received. Her face made him think of the statue of the Madonna in the church where he'd grown up—sweet and purely carved.

"Let me show you your room," he said briskly. "Tonio! Grab the bag." He barked out other orders and the boys scurried to obey.

All except Zach, an eight-year-old with a bristly blond flattop and a smattering of freckles across his sullen face.

"What's up, Zach?" Ramón asked.

The boy tucked his thumbs into his jeans and stared at Tanya. "Nothin'," he said.

"Have you done your chores?" Tonio asked, coming up behind the adults.

"You're not the boss of me," Zach snarled.

Ramón frowned. The child was fairly new—he'd only been there for a little more than two weeks—and had come to the ranch only after his sixteenth arrest, when no foster homes would take him. A hard case, but he was so young, Ramón intended to keep him awhile if he could. "Zach, is there something on your mind?"

His flat, hostile gaze flickered over Tanya, then to Tonio. "He's always telling me what to do. Damn Goody Two-shoes."

Ramón gave Tanya an apologetic lift of the brows. To Tonio, he said, "Son, show Ms. Bishop to her room, please."

"Sure." The long-legged teenager opened the door. "Right this way."

Tanya gave Ramón a single, terrified glance, then took a breath and followed her son.

Ramón waited until they had gone inside, then remained silent a moment longer, watching Zach carefully. The boy was very upset about something. He was fighting tears even as they stood there. "Are you having some problem, Zach? You want to tell me about it?"

Zach wavered a moment, then lifted his head and uttered an obscenity that more or less told Ramón to get lost.

Ramón sighed. "I hope you had a good lunch, son—"

"I'm not your son! I'm not anybody's son! Leave me alone!"

When he would have bolted from the porch, Ramón grabbed him firmly by the arm. Holding on just above the elbow, he headed for the dorms, Zach cursing and tugging all the way. "You know the rules, Zach. If you swear, you'll go to bed with no supper. I hate to do it, but you leave me no choice."

A dark, burly man met them at the door of the dorms. "Zach will not be dining with us tonight," Ramón said. "Will you see him to his room, Mr. Mahaney?"

"I'm real sorry to hear that, Zach."

The boy, out of control now, swore again. The two men exchanged grips. "Mozart tonight, I think," Ramón said, smiling.

"Good choice," David Mahaney said.

* * *

Tanya followed Tonio into the house. Her heart raced with a sick speed, making her feel almost faint. When the edges of her vision grew dark, she stopped abruptly, forcing herself to breathe in slow, steady breaths. It would not make a nice impression to hyperventilate and faint in the hall.

Tonio stopped and turned around. "You okay?"

Tanya nodded, breathing slowly, her hand on a carved wooden post. "It's just been a long day," she said.

He smiled, and it wasn't phoney or falsely patient. "I'll have Desmary bring you some coffee or something."

"No, that's all right," she said, straightening. "I'm fine."

"Sure?"

Oh, Ramón, you've done a fine, fine job! Tanya smiled. "Very."

By the time he'd led the way up a wide, sweeping staircase to the third floor of the old farmhouse, Tanya had calmed considerably. He showed her into a gracious, turn-of-the-century room with wide windows overlooking the semiarid land. Sea foam green wallpaper graced the angles made by the dormers, and a handmade quilt in green and white covered the bed. For a single moment, Tanya could not quite believe this would be her room.

With a surprising lack of self-consciousness, Tonio pointed out the bathroom down the hall, the linen closet and various other amenities. She drank in the resonant tenor of his voice and found hints of the three-year-old she'd left behind.

But she could not study him the way she wished to, not now. She couldn't seem too curious or strange, so it would have to be done in bits. His voice, his easy movements—those were enough for now.

"Thanks," she said, finally, knowing she should let him go. "I'll be fine."

"See you at dinner," Tonio said amiably, and left, shutting the door behind him.

Tanya sank down on the bed, alone in the quiet for the first time since she could remember. Even at the halfway house, there had been constant noise—the sound of a radio or a telephone or people talking, and the rooms had been only one step above the cells at the prison. Here, the quilt was soft with many washings and smelled faintly of dusting powder. With a sense of sybaritic freedom, Tanya closed her eyes and pulled the quilt around her, drowning in the deliciousness.

This was what she had missed, more than anything. Pure solitude, and silence. For several long moments, she reveled in it, drowned in it, and then was startled by a knock at the door. "Just a minute!" she called.

It was Antonio, back again, a stack of magazines in his hands. "Don't tell my dad I forgot these," he said, sheepishly. "I was supposed to put them in here before you got here and I forgot."

Tanya smiled and accepted the stack. "The *New Yorker?*" she said in a puzzled voice. "Interesting."

Tonio inclined his head, putting his hands on his hips. "Yeah, well, Dad's got this thing about magazines. Everybody has magazines in their rooms—weird stuff, all of it, like that."

Tanya sensed he wasn't in a hurry to go, and held the magazines loosely against her chest. As if she were only lazily making conversation, she flipped the top magazine against her and asked, "Where do they come from?"

"In the mail. We get like twenty magazines and newspapers a week. The postman has to make a special trip."

Tanya lifted her head and smiled. "He has an unusual approach to things, doesn't he?"

"Yeah." He shrugged. "Yeah, he's a good guy once you get through all his weirdness."

"Weird?" Now she noticed the beautiful slant of her son's eyes, the deep clear blue framed with extraordinarily long, sooty lashes. As a baby, those lashes had swept over half his cheeks when he slept. No old lady in the world could resist him. "He doesn't seem weird to me."

Tonio gave her a tilted smile, and the expression was rakish, even in a fourteen-year-old. "You'll see." There was fondness in his tone. "He's not like anybody else."

Tanya nodded. "Thanks. I won't tell you forgot."

"Desmary said you can come on down whenever you want."

"Thanks," she said again, and her hope that everything would be all right soared. Cheerfully, she changed her clothes and went down the stairs to the kitchen, humming softly under her breath.

For the most part, it didn't look as if much of the farmhouse had been altered. As she passed through the rooms of the ground floor—living room, library, what surely once would have been called a parlor, and dining room with a fireplace—she noticed the fine detail work that was the hallmark of turn-of-the-century craftsmen. All had been lovingly preserved.

Even in the kitchen, attempts had been made to keep the original flavor of the old house. A broad bank of windows looked toward the barns, and a big butcher-block table dominated the center of the room.

There the quaintness ended and the stainless steel began. Industrial-size refrigerators banked one wall, and below the windows were deep, functional sinks adjacent to a huge dishwasher in the corner.

Stirring the contents of a big pot was an old woman, almost whimsically misplaced in the gleaming kitchen. She turned at the sound of Tanya's feet on the linoleum floor, and Tanya was reminded of dolls made from apples. Her pale brown face was seamed deeply around snapping, alert blue eyes. A flour-dusted red apron covered a plump figure, and gray-and-white braids touched her hips. "Hi," Tanya said, a little shyly. "You must be Desmary."

"Hello, Tanya!" Her voice was both robust and kind. "I've been waiting to meet you. Come in and sit down."

"Oh, I'd rather help you get supper on the table, if I may."

"Today, you just watch how I do things." She pointed with a wooden spoon to the banks of cupboards along one wall. "Poke around and find out where things are, and you'll be more of a help than a hindrance tomorrow." She smiled over her shoulder.

Tanya chuckled. "Okay." Still a little hesitant, she rounded the room, opening doors and cupboards and drawers. "How long have you worked here?" she asked, memorizing the organization of the refrigerator and freezer.

"I've been a cook all my life," she said, and Tanya caught a hint of a lilt to her words. Irish or perhaps Scottish, but a long time in the past. "I've been cookin' for Ramón and his boys since he opened up the ranch to them."

"Do you like it?"

"Aye." She gestured toward the drawers. "Fetch me a slotted spoon from that top one, will you?"

Tanya hurried to comply. As Desmary turned to take the utensil, Tanya saw the rolling, limping gait of very bad feet, and nearly offered to fetch a stool as well, but remembered in time that Ramón had asked her to be discreet. Instead, she pointed through a set of double doors to a long, open room set with small, family-size tables. "Is that where everyone eats?"

"The boys and the counselors eat there," she said. "The rest of us use the other dining room—you'll eat with us." Lifting chicken pieces from broth, she added, "Ramón would give everything to the boys. But I told him he needs to have a time he isn't with them."

Tanya smiled. "You take care of him, then."

"Aye, since he has no wife or mother to do it." She gave Tanya a mischievous grin. "Men can't do it by themselves, as I'm sure you're aware."

The back door opened and as if their conversation had called him, Ramón strode in. Tanya noticed again the sense of energy that surrounded him, a vigor she found deeply appealing. "Ah, you've met! Good."

"Aye, we've met, no thanks to you, lad." Desmary turned, her movements as laborious as before, and Tanya caught Ramón's eye above the old woman's head. Quick knowledge passed between them— Tanya would happily share his cause to protect and make comfortable this delightful woman.

He joined them beside the stove and reached for a shred of chicken, which he popped into his mouth before Desmary could slap his hand. "Not bad," he said with a wink toward Tanya. "Needs salt."

"Leave my food alone, boy, or I'll feed you porridge for dinner."

Ramón chuckled. "No, you won't, old woman," he said, touching her shoulder fondly. "I brought you a helper today."

He touched Tanya's shoulder, too. The gesture was meant to be inclusive and comforting, and she could tell from even such short acquaintance that Ramón was the sort of man who touched people easily and often.

She told herself all those things, feeling the light, friendly grip of that beautiful, long-fingered hand against her skin. But reason warred with emotion, and even the emotions warred with each other. In eleven years, she'd not been touched in friendliness, and her first impulse was to pull away violently, as she had at the bus station. She quelled the impulse by staring at the piles of steaming chicken on a plate.

Ramón's fingers moved on her shoulder and on Desmary's. Inclusive, gentle, meant to comfort. She swallowed, hearing only the voices that flowed around her in easy camaraderie as a second emotion swelled through her: need. Not need as in desire, although his warm palm sparked the same rustling of cinders she'd experienced earlier. No, this need was more dangerous even than desire. It was the oldest and most devastating need of the human spirit, the need to be enfolded, held close to the heart and soul of another, mingling comfort and quiet and...

Pressing her lips together, she eased away from him, pretending to need to find something from a drawer. When she looked up, Ramón was gazing at her silently, a measuring expression in his dark eyes.

Hastily, she looked away, wondering how in the world she was going to gird herself to resist him.

Chapter Three

Dear Antonio,

I've taken up running. It's strange to be doing it—me, who could never play any sport, who was always the last one chosen for a game in school—but I love it. I love moving in the morning air, feeling the wind cool my hot skin. I love the taste of morning on my tongue. But mostly, I like feeling strong. I like feeling as if no one could catch me unless I wanted them to.

Maybe if I'd learned to run before this, you and I would be running somewhere together. Maybe I'd be the one taking you to first grade, instead of your uncle Ramón. Maybe—

No, thinking that way makes a person crazy. I love running. I'm glad I found it. Perhaps one day, you and I will have a chance to run on a track or in a park somewhere. Anywhere. Be good, *hijo*.

Love, Mom

Dinner that first night was awkward. Tanya ate with Ramón and Tonio and Desmary in the warm, wood-trimmed dining room with its built-in buffet and lace curtains hanging at the windows. She tried to appear alert and interested in the conversation, but the truth was, waves of exhaustion and emotion—shock, joy, and if she allowed it, attraction—rocked her.

Putting peas on her plate, she tried to ignore that last thought and the way it sneaked in, like a boy in the trunk of a car at a drive-in movie. She couldn't allow herself the luxury of even considering Ramón Quezada attractive. She couldn't let herself be that vulnerable.

In prison, she had learned to stay alert, to live in the moment. It had been the only way she could quell the periodic attacks of panic she experienced there. By focusing on the very instant in which she found herself, she could manage anything. Such an approach helped her handle terrible things by taking them one at a time. It also gave her an ability to treasure the joyous moments, to really be present in them when they happened. Taking in a calming, deep breath, she looked around. In this moment she saw Tonio at fourteen, his hair black and gleaming, his teeth even and big and white in his planed face. A beautiful man-child who'd once shared her very blood. He shared this moment with her, after so many years of her wishing it could be so.

A miracle.

At the edge of her peripheral vision, Ramón laughed. She saw his long, dark throat move with his pleasure, saw his lips turn up, his teeth shine white.

Tanya willed her focus to the other side of the table, where Desmary sat, her hair gone wispy with the heat of the kitchen, her apple-doll face shadowed in the low light. Tanya knew she would like the old woman.

But women were always easier. She understood women. Men had such different signals and ways of being. Their customs and language were a thing apart.

Ramón moved. Tanya glanced over, and watched as he bent to give a tidbit of food to a cat who waited patiently at the side of his chair. The cat delicately accepted the morsel from his long fingers, and Ramón patiently waited until the cat was finished before he straightened.

He caught her gaze and gave her a sheepish grin. "Sorry about that. Do you hate to see animals fed from the table? I know a lot of people don't like it."

"I don't mind," she said. "I never had pets."

"Never?" Tonio echoed. As if stunned, he looked around the room. A border collie slept by the door, a canary sang in a corner, and the tortoiseshell cat kept vigil at Ramón's chair. "How sad."

Tanya smiled. "It was. I'm glad I can get to know so many animals here."

Ramón chuckled. "I think Merlin would be a good dog for Tanya, don't you? He likes women a lot."

"Merlin?"

"I bet we won't even have to introduce you," Ramón said. "Merlin will find you." A twinkle shone in his dark eyes. "He's a character, I warn you."

The chuckle and the twinkle and his mesmerizing voice combined to envelope Tanya in a powerful field of sexual awareness. It was bold and clear and true—and all the more overwhelming because it had been so long since she'd experienced the feeling. With effort, she looked away. "I'll look forward to it," she mumbled.

Focus, she told herself. Candles burned in old brass candlesticks on the mantel, their flames reflecting in the high mirror over the fireplace. A small table by the hearth held a very elaborate chess set, made of carved silver-and-brass figures set with faux jewels. A woman had made this room, she thought, and wondered who. Ramón's mother? Grandmother? A sister?

On the table were handmade rolls and a bowl of peas and a nice slab of roast beef, and a pot of coffee and a pitcher of water.

Tanya tried to keep her focus on those things, but every time she turned her head even a little, there he

was again, filling her vision. It astonished her that
he'd grown so fully into himself, so rich a feast for her
senses that she could barely stand to look at him.

Focus. On Antonio. Her son. What an amazing
thought that was sometimes! She liked his voice. Not
too deep, not too high—a pleasant tenor faintly lilt-
ing with a southwest accent. That accent had de-
lighted her upon her arrival in Albuquerque so many
years ago, and it would have surprised her deeply if
he'd escaped it. He spoke now of his girlfriend, Teresa, who was fourteen and very smart.

Tanya smiled at that. "Does she get good grades?"
she asked, buttering a roll.

"No. She's not real good at school but she's smart
about everything. She knows stuff." He brightened.
"She likes to read."

It was impossible to avoid sharing a smile with Ramón over that. He'd been so impressed with her taste
in reading—and Tanya hadn't even known enough to
know she was slowly working her way through most
of the classics of the English language. She just read
because she liked it, because books were safe and took
her away from the strains of daily life.

And not even Victor could be jealous of a book.

Ramón winked at her. His expression was gentle
and kind, his fathomless eyes like the night sky, endless and vast beyond all imagining. He had a great
face, Tanya thought, admiring again the cut of
cheekbones, the high-bridged nose and elegantly

carved nostrils. She avoided his mouth this time. It
was just too—well, *sexy.*

As if he sensed her thoughts, something in his face
changed. It was slight and almost indefinable, but
definite. It was a penetrating expression that made her
aware of her female parts. Aware of her skin, and her
limbs. It made her aware, too, of *his* skin and limbs
and male parts.

The thought was unexpected and oddly erotic.
Trying to appear composed, she reached for the bowl
of mashed potatoes. The bowl was not a problem, but
she had terrible trouble grasping the spoon between
her thumb and forefinger. It was only a matter of
seconds, but it seemed like hours before she could
hold it properly and ladle potatoes on her plate.

"This food is wonderful, Desmary," she said. Her
voice croaked a little. Embarrassed, she vowed to be
quiet, and keep her eyes to herself.

In a few days, she'd be used to everything, she told
herself. She'd be used to the smells of the farmhouse, age and cooking and maleness. She'd be used
to the sound of Ramón's voice, rich with inflections,
rolling around her like a musical composition. She'd
be used to catching sight of Antonio, blue-eyed and
dark and so beautiful.

Feeling close to tears, she put her fork carefully
beside her plate and looked at Ramón. "I think I'm
very tired. I'd like to go to my room."

A flicker of concern touched his eyes. "Are you all
right?"

"Yes." She stood. "It's just been a very long day."

Ramón put his napkin aside. "I'll walk up with you."

"No. Please, just enjoy your dinner."

"I'll be back in a minute, Desmary. Don't let the boys take my plate."

His solicitousness made her feel even more vulnerable, and therefore panicky. She'd spent too many long years learning how to hide her feelings, how to appear strong when she felt like a marshmallow inside.

But in all that time, she'd not had to confront her past in such concrete ways. Nor had she been attracted to anyone. In fact, she'd believed that part of her dead forever until she'd seen Ramón standing on the platform this afternoon.

Now he stood there, beautiful and kind, holding out one long-fingered brown hand toward her. "I'm okay," she said, and bolted.

She ran all the way to her room on the third floor and slammed the door closed. The soft, soft bed with its piles of pillows looked as inviting as a mother's arms. She kicked off her shoes and dived into the comforting mass, making a cocoon of pillows and coverlet, shutting out all thought with the same picture that had given her comfort so many nights in prison...a simple open meadow, surrounded with tall pines. In the middle of it was a tent. Her tent. When she went in, nothing could harm her.

Thus comforted, she fell asleep.

* * *

Ramón cursed himself as Tanya ran away from him. Once again, he'd frightened her. It was going to be a lot more difficult than he thought to learn his way around her.

She didn't reappear that evening, and just before he turned in, Ramón knocked on her door, softly. Light spilled out from below it, and he knocked again, a little louder, when she didn't answer.

Still no sound from beyond. Concerned, he pursed his lips and weighed his choices. Although she'd tried to seem calm, he'd seen her distress earlier, and he knew he wouldn't sleep until he found out she was all right. He knocked again, firmly. Again, no answer.

He could go down the stairs and get Desmary, but that would mean making the old woman walk up three flights of stairs on her bad feet. He didn't have the heart. There were no other women in the house.

But what if he opened the door and Tanya wasn't dressed?

He'd just peek in, carefully. If she was all right, he'd just close the door and go on his way. If not, he'd be glad he looked in on her.

Turning the handle very slowly, he pushed the door open a crack and peered inside. For a moment, he could see no sign of her at all. Then he spied her, on the bed and mostly dressed.

She was sound asleep. A small snore wheezed in and out of her slightly parted lips. She'd evidentially started out curled in the covers, but the house was warm, and she'd flung parts of the covers off. Her shirt was unbuttoned a little, and a swell of breast spilled from the opening, as if anxious to be freed. One arm and one bare leg were uncovered.

Ramón stood at the bedside admiring her with a feeling he couldn't quite identify. How many times had he thought of her sleeping in the cold, dead confines of a prison cot while he lay alone in a double bed, a pillow clasped to his chest? How many times had he wondered how time had changed her, molded her?

Every day. Every day he had thought of her.

As he stood there, she turned, muttering to herself, and a spill of hair fell over her face. Gently, he reached out to push it away, unwilling to leave her alone just yet. He wanted to just watch her sleep, knowing she was finally safe here.

His touch startled her. She came awake with an eerie, sharp suddenness, sitting straight up and bumping his mouth with her head. He made a noise and moved back, bringing his fingers to his lip, and tasted blood. He stumbled backward, out of her way.

She blinked, staring at him, at her room in disorientation. Slowly, she seemed to get her bearings, and Ramón felt guilty for disturbing her. "What are you doing in here?" she asked at last.

"I was worried about you."

Tanya rubbed her head, eyeing his mouth. "I'd suggest in the future that you don't touch me when you wake me up. Just say my name."

"No problem." He gave her a rueful smile. "Sorry. Soon enough you won't need a worrywart checking on you."

She rubbed her face, pulling back her hair in an unconsciously sexy gesture that put her breasts in relief against the lamplight shining through her blouse. He looked away, but his gaze snagged on her bare knees, smooth and neat-looking. He backed toward the door. "I'll leave you alone now," he said.

She looked at him soberly. "I'm sorry about the way I left the dinner table, Ramón. I just got scared all of a sudden."

"I know," he said. All at once, he was struck with her isolation here. Who did she have to lean on in this new time of her life?

Who had she ever had?

Ramón pointed to the bed, nearby her. "Do you mind if I sit down for a minute?"

The smallest hesitation marked her response. "No," she said quietly. "No, I don't mind."

He sat down next to her. Felt the warmth of her leg against his own. "You're as jumpy as a cricket," he said, looking at her. "What scares you the most?"

She gazed up at him steadily for a minute, and in the dark blue waters of her eyes, he saw a thousand moving thoughts. "You," she said at last. "You scare me."

The answer was so unexpected, Ramón found himself speechless. Finally he asked, "Why me?"

But the first honesty had been all she could manage. With a diffident lift of her shoulder, she looked at her hands. "I don't know."

He ached to put his arm around her, as he would one of the lost boys he took in. He wanted to hold her until the cold places inside her could thaw. But he'd seen her reaction to his touch earlier and knew it would take some time before she could allow her walls to be breached.

Instead, he bent almost sideways to look into her face from an exaggeratedly silly angle. "I'm a clown, *grilla*. You don't have to be afraid of me."

"Gria?"

"Cricket," he said, smiling.

A reluctant grin touched her mouth, and he saw a flash of the impossibly young girl he'd danced with at a wedding reception so long ago. "No, I'm not afraid of you like that. I know you aren't mean," she said.

He knew what she meant, but didn't know if it should be acknowledged between them or left to lie. Acting out of pure instinct, he said, "Ah, you mean because I'm so gorgeous!"

It was the right thing to say. She laughed. "Yes. That's it."

"Well, don't worry," he said briskly, and patted her knee. Standing to take his leave, he winked. "It happens to all the girls. You'll get used to it."

The open, trusting smile on her face just then was worth anything. He wished with all of himself that he could bend and put his mouth to hers, that he could taste that sweet smile.

But he could no more do it now than he could have done it fifteen years ago. Before he could be further tempted, he bowed with a flourish. "Good night, Tanya."

"Good night, Ramón."

Ten days later, in the crisp ghostly air of early October, Tanya stepped onto the wooden porch of the farmhouse. Above the Sangre de Cristos, pale dawn had begun to bleed the night from the sky. Tanya gazed at the peaks as she methodically stretched her calves and arches and hamstrings, getting ready for her morning run.

Around the corner from the barns came a dog. It was gold and white, with patches of gray. One of the counselors said he was a blue heeler mix with more good nature than good sense. She didn't care if he wasn't smart—he'd run with her every day so far, and his companionship was one of the most pleasant things she'd ever discovered.

"Good morning, Merlin," Tanya said, moving from side to side to stretch her spine. He lifted his nose at her and sat at the bottom of the steps to wait.

Her days since her arrival had settled into a pattern. Mornings she ran her usual three miles, then got back in time to shower and help Desmary get breakfast on the table before the bus came for the boys who had clearance to go to public school. The rest went to classes held in rooms set aside for such purposes in the dorms.

The days she spent working with Desmary and whatever boys happened to be on KP that week or just drifted in to sit at the table and steal nibbles of carrot or apple or cake batter. Sometimes Tonio was one of them.

They seemed so hungry to just sit in the kitchen with the women that Tanya asked Desmary about it.

"They miss their mothers," Desmary had replied simply.

"You ready, Merlin?" Tanya skipped down the steps and paused to scratch the dog's ears. He made a soft, whining yip to signal his impatience.

"Come on, then," she said with a laugh.

Tanya began to run loosely, past the barns and the corrals, the pens with their sheep, the vast gardens with tangles of yellowing squash and melon vines, and pepper and tomato plants still heavily laden with fruit. Behind them grew stands of corn.

The air tasted like leaf smoke, and Tanya smiled, thinking it had been a long time since she'd smelled that particular aroma. Out here, some agricultural burning was allowed.

Her body fell into its natural, loping rhythm. She didn't run fast, just steadfastly. This morning, she took particular joy in the sturdy new running shoes on her feet. They had cost almost half her first paycheck, but even after one day, Tanya could feel the difference. In the prison yard, where she'd run in the grass along the perimeters of the fence, a pair of ordinary sneakers had been fine. Here there were cacti and thorny goatheads and the possibility of snakes, and she'd quickly seen the need for better shoes.

Aside from the protection they offered from pointy invasions, they made her feet feel embraced. Bouncing, she tested the sensations once again. A hug around her arch, a cushion under the balls of her feet. Quite luxurious.

She'd also purchased a pair of sweats and a sweatshirt in dark blue, and she was grateful for their warmth this chilly morning. Her cheeks tingled with a sharp breeze sweeping down from the northern mountains.

Merlin crisscrossed the path in front of her like a vigilant scout, and it made her feel safe. The fine thin mountain air tasted as cool and sweet as apples, and she breathed in with gratitude.

Glorious.

As a girl, Tanya had never been athletic. She was hopelessly incapable of doing anything with a ball, whether it be basket, bowling or tennis balls. There was just some short circuit in her brain that made it impossible for her. In school she'd suffered endless humiliations at the hands of gestapo teachers and cruel classmates. She flunked PE her junior year and vowed she'd never go back.

And she hadn't.

In prison, however, she'd discovered the deep pleasure of solitary noncompetitive exercise. At first, she'd simply walked the perimeters of the yard, over and over and over, walking away her grief and fury so she wouldn't lose her mind inside the walls of he cell. That had gone on for a long time, her restless, endless walking. One day, almost crazy with missing her son, she bent her head down and leaned into a run. When she stopped twenty minutes later, her heart pounding, her breath ragged, she had felt a strange peace.

Sometimes, she didn't feel like running, so she walked. Sometimes she didn't feel like even walking, but she did it anyway. Over a long, long time, her body had grown lean and ropy, like the body of an antelope, and she moved with·a loose freedom she'd never known. Running made her strong.

She and Merlin made their circle and returned to the main buildings just as the sun came over the horizon. At the barn, she slowed to a walk to let her body cool down, feeling a pleasant tingle in her limbs, as if her blood were seltzer. Next to her, Merlin gave a little dancing leap and licked her fingers. She patted his head. "Good dog."

When she came into the yard near the house, she saw Ramón standing on the porch. He wore jeans and well-used riding boots, a black jean jacket and a flannel shirt. Ready for a day in the yard, she thought calmly. But it was only attempted calm. She couldn't catch a glimpse of him without feeling a small, electric charge at the sensual promise of that face, that mouth, those hands. To hide her discomfort, she tugged the fat band out of her hair and shook her hair loose. "Good morning," she said.

"Did you have a good run?"

"Yes." She smiled. "Always."

He didn't say anything more, but Tanya could sense there was something on his mind. At last he said, "There is going to be a harvest dance here. I wonder if you would help me plan it."

Tanya gaped. "A dance?"

"Yes. The boys can ask girls from school. We'll clear the dining room and let one of the kids play DJ. Serve food." He smiled. "You know. A dance."

For one small moment, Tanya looked at him, remembering the reception at which she had danced with him so long ago. Remembered the feeling of his strong, lean arms around her, the press of his flat stomach against her swelling one. How odd, she thought now, that the child in her at that moment had gone to him for safekeeping. "I don't know a lot about that kind of thing," she said at last. "Next to nothing. I got married pretty young."

"I know." He cocked his head in a purely Latin gesture, lifting one shoulder at the same time. "We can learn together."

It would be churlish to refuse. He'd been nothing but kind to her. "All right."

His smile—white and fast in his dark face—flashed suddenly. It struck her as forcefully as always, right in the knees. A tingling that had nothing to do with her run crept through private parts of her body.

"Good." He shifted to let her pass on the steps. "Be ready about 2:00 and we can go into town for some books."

"Town?" she echoed. She'd been very, very careful to avoid his company. A cozy little ride into town didn't seem exactly the best idea. "I—"

"You haven't been to the library yet. You'll like it." His gaze was steady, fathomless. Somehow Tanya knew that he sensed all her objections and silenced them. "See you at 2:00."

There was nothing to say to that. Tanya gave him a half smile of capitulation. "Okay."

He gave her a wink and headed toward the barns. Into the quiet air rang his jaunty, tuneful whistle, and Tanya had to smile. He was the most relentlessly good-natured man she'd ever met. In ten days, she'd never heard him raise his voice or snap at a child, or get annoyed with a task. Relentlessly good-natured.

But as she watched him walk away, Tanya had to admit it was not his nature upon which she feasted her eyes. He had a rear end like a quarterback, taut and high and round.

"You gonna stand there all mornin' watching his behind," Desmary said in a droll tone from the back door, "or you gonna come help me cook sometime today?"

Tanya gave a quick laugh and turned around, aware her color was high. The old woman winked. "I'm still inclined to admire it myself." She gave a quick flick of her head toward the interior of the house. "Go get your shower. I'm all right for a little while."

"Thanks."

Chapter Four

Dear Antonio,

One of the last warm days of the year. I spent the last few days roasting and peeling chilies, and my fingers are blistered. I don't mind, though. I love the smell of them roasting.

I wonder what foods you like to eat. When you were a baby, you ate so many strawberries you got allergic to them. And you liked pork and beans and McDonald's hamburgers and candy. But you were still so little then, it isn't like big kid eating. Like having your own set of favorites and dislikes that isn't like anyone else's. I hate egg whites, you know that? And milk and okra. I

love chilies and tomatoes and lots of fresh vegetables. I'm pretty good in the kitchen, too. That's
where I've been working lately. It's a good place.

You be sure to eat all your vegetables. They
give you clear skin and good vision and strong
bones.

                                        Love, Mom

After breakfast, Tanya chopped vegetables for the
stew they would all eat for supper—fresh green peppers, some late cabbage and broccoli, and tender
fresh carrots. Desmary, sitting on her high stool,
gazed out the window as she kneaded bread on the
counter. Tanya hummed softly a tune from childhood, about a woman who got married the day before she died.

"That's such a happy sound, that humming,"
Desmary said, flashing a smile over her shoulder.
"Makes me think of my youth."

Tanya grinned. "Not everyone shares your enjoy-
ment. I've been told very bluntly to shut up."

"People just get used to things being a certain way.
The kids now, they don't have people sing to them.
Their mothers turn on the radio when they do chores.
Mine used to sing." With a deft move of her wrists,
she flipped the bread dough twist and looked at
Tanya. "'Amazing Grace.'"

From the short hallway that led to the communal
dining room for the boys and the counselors came a

child. It was the same little boy who'd been on the porch the day of Tanya's arrival. His name was Zach and he was in trouble almost all the time, and Tanya felt sorry for him. She had asked if he could be assigned to the kitchen more often, and the counselors had only been too happy to do it. For some reason, Zach calmed a little in her presence.

In his arms he carried a basket of green Anaheim peppers, long and shiny and freshly picked. Behind him came a second boy and two counselors, all bearing bushels of peppers. Desmary caught sight of them and made a noise of frustration. "I haven't seen so many peppers in one season in years!" She put her knife down and came over, her rolling gait obviously more painful than usual. With a gnarled finger, she poked the flesh of the peppers and sighed. "They have to get done right away. We'll have the apples to do this weekend."

"Apples?" Tanya echoed.

With a gloomy look, Desmary nodded. "We'll sell most of them, but some get put up in cider and butter." She snapped her fingers in annoyance. "Which reminds me—I've got to get Ramón to pick up some canning jars for me."

Tanya looked at the piles of peppers and realized she couldn't leave Desmary to fend for herself. She couldn't possibly go with Ramón to town this afternoon. She wasn't sure if she was disappointed or relieved.

To the counselors, she said, "We need a few boys to peel chilies this evening. Can you send about four or five over after supper?"

David winked. "Sure." He touched Zach's head. "Come on, kid."

Zach shot the man a glowering look and didn't move. His bristly blond flattop had been recently trimmed and stood at rigid attention over the top of his head. Freckles dotted his small nose.

"Can I keep him in here a little while?" Tanya asked. "I need some help getting these washed."

"I guess it won't hurt. Zach, you'll be in reading class in an hour—are we clear?"

"Yessir."

The counselors left. Desmary peered at the table with a look of great doom on her face. "I hate chilies," she said. "What kind of fool vegetable is that, anyway? One that burns you?"

Tanya touched her shoulder. "I'll take care of them. Why don't you take a little rest?"

"No, you need help this morning."

"No I don't." Gently, she turned Desmary around. "I'll get Ramón in here to help me with lunch. Zach is going to help me with washing the chilies, and I can get them roasted this afternoon. The boys will peel them tonight."

Desmary looked at Tanya for a long moment. "You're supposed to go to town with Ramón today."

She shrugged. "We'll go tomorrow. And I'll get you some canning jars."

Moving with deep stiffness, Desmary removed her apron and limped toward her rooms. "Call me if you need anything."

"We'll be fine," Tanya said, giving Zach a wink.

When they were alone, she lifted a bushel basket of chilies and carried them to the big stainless steel sink. "You bring them over here, Zach, and I'll wash."

"Okay."

"What are you doing home this morning?"

He carefully put the basket at her feet and straightened. "Got suspended yesterday."

"Uh-oh." Giving him an exaggerated frown over her shoulder, Tanya turned on the water in the sink and upturned a basket of chilies. "What happened?"

"That jerk Jimmy Trujillo called me names again."

"And you got suspended?"

A frown drew his sandy-colored brows into a V. "No. I hit him and broke one of his teeth."

"Didn't that hurt your hand?"

Zach leaned forward. "Look," he said, pointing to a gash on his knuckles. "That's what happened."

Very seriously, Tanya took the proffered hand and peered at the cut. It was healing nicely, but she hung on to his hand while she patted her apron pocket. "I think you need a bandage."

"Naw," Zach protested, but he didn't pull away.

Tanya located a Band-Aid—she kept them there for the small cutting knife wounds that inexperienced cooks naturally acquired—and covered the gash on Zach's knuckles. Still she didn't let go, examining his fingers and palm. "Your hands are getting chapped. You need to keep lotion on them."

"Okay." He leaned on the counter to watch her wash the chilies. "Whatcha gonna do with those?"

"Roast and peel them," she said.

"Can I help?"

"For a little while." Tanya looked at the clock. "You mustn't forget your class."

"I won't," he promised.

Tanya smiled at him, feeling a warm stir touch her heart. "I know."

Ramón found himself rushing through his chores, anxious to get everything done in time to give himself a little break this afternoon with Tanya. For several days, he'd been searching for an excuse to be with her for a few hours—just to see how she was adjusting.

Yeah, right.

He sucked in a breath. Truth was, this morning she'd been almost more gorgeous than a woman had a right to be, her hair swinging, her color high with her exercise, her legs hard beneath the sweats, her breasts moving under the—

No, he'd leave that thought alone.

Pounding a nail into the broken bit of fence he was mending, Ramón cursed. It wasn't as if he hadn't had his share of women, although he did have to be discreet. In order to provide a good example, he didn't stay out all night or bring women out here to sleep with him.

Not that a man had to stay out all night to have his needs met. But the truth was, Ramón didn't like to have sex casually. It always seemed to him sex was too intimate and revealing for anything except the deepest of relationships. Last spring, he'd broken off a long-term relationship with a teacher in Manzanares when she had finally admitted she didn't think she could stand to live at the ranch with all those boys and still pursue her own career in teaching as well as raise kids of her own. He'd understood, and had not been particularly brokenhearted. Their relationship had been close and well matched, but had there ever really been a fire?

Slam, slam, slam. He pounded nails into the fence, scaring a pair of quails from a nearby scrub oak. They flittered into the morning with noises of surprise and alarm.

Ten days Tanya had been here. Only ten days, and already Ramón had started spinning naughty fantasies about her naked body. Which would have been all right except for a couple of small details.

The most difficult aspect of the whole thing was that she was Tonio's mother—and Tonio didn't know that. When and if he found out, if they felt right about revealing that to him, things might go well or they might not. If Tonio felt betrayed—and the possibility definitely existed—then Ramón's first obligation was to Tonio. It had to be.

He took a nail from the bag around his waist and positioned it. Tonio had been told his mother's story... and professed an understanding of it, but Ramón knew the understanding was purely intellectual. Emotionally, the boy still felt his mother hadn't wanted him. Only time and maturity could change that.

The other problem was much larger and had to do with Tanya herself. When Ramón met her, she'd been eighteen and pregnant. She and Victor had been together for more than three years even then—since a fourteen-year-old Tanya had moved to Albuquerque. At nineteen, she'd divorced him. At barely twenty-two, after more than two solid years of being stalked unceasingly, Tanya had killed him.

And went to prison.

Eleven years later, the girl was a woman, but a woman who'd never had a chance to experience the full freedom of adulthood. Living on her own, making her own choices, being in charge of everything. He wanted her to have that if she wanted it. He didn't want to take advantage of her trust in him, or her gratitude to him for caring for Antonio all these years. What he wanted was impossible—an unencumbered Tanya and unfettered Ramón to meet when he was twenty-three and she was twenty. He wanted to go back in time, to rescue her from her nightmare before it ruined her life.

Impossible.

He stopped pounding and looked at the bright blue New Mexico sky above the dun and red and sage of the land. Was he chasing some dream of the past? Was he acting out of guilt? Were his feelings even genuine?

He didn't know. Until he did, he'd do his best to keep his physical attraction to himself. There was no reason in the world they couldn't just be friends for now. It was the best choice.

A boy on horseback approached. "Mr. Quezada, they need you in the kitchen."

"Did they say why?"

The boy grinned. "They've got chilies to the ceiling. Ms. Bishop says she can't go to town today, but maybe you could come help with the chilies."

Ramón was aware of a sharp, pricking sense of disappointment in his chest. But he nodded. "Thanks, Porfie."

With Ramón's help, Tanya got lunch on the table and cleaned up without incident. Afterward, they started roasting chilies.

Tanya peeked into the oven, careful to keep her face back from the wave of heat that rolled out. The chilies swelled and made tiny noises as steam escaped from within, the green tubes rising and falling as air escaped. The skin was beginning to toast, but this batch wasn't quite done.

From behind her, almost directly at her shoulder, Ramón said, "They look like they're breathing, don't they?"

She looked at the chilies again. Rising and falling, like little green lungs. "I never noticed that before. You're right."

"They scream, too—listen."

A soft high sound of escaping air slowly filtered from the chilies. Tanya straightened with an exaggerated wince of horror. "Yuck!"

He stood rather close, close enough for her arm to brush his as she stood up, but he didn't move away. "I used to run away and hide in my room when my *abuelita* roasted chilies. I think someone should write a story about the chili monster for kids in the Southwest."

Tanya smiled up at him, drawing warm pleasure from the sense of his body so close to hers. On his chin, there was a tiny nick from his morning shave. She wanted to touch it. "Maybe you should write one," she said lightly.

A starry twinkle lit his irises. "Maybe I should." With mock seriousness, he drew his brows together. "I'll call him Diablo Chili, and give him a big shaggy mustache. He'll be one of those monsters that drag themselves up the stairs at night, panting."

"I'm never going to eat chilies again!" Tanya protested.

He laughed. "Sure you will. Smell that!"

Aware that she hadn't moved, Tanya bowed her head and shifted away, reaching automatically for the next batch of chilies and spreading them over a foil-covered cookie sheet.

"So how bad is Desmary?" Ramón asked, moving to lean one hip against the sink.

"I think she's just tired. She's resting." As if she didn't mind, as if it were nothing at all, Tanya glanced at him. "I hope you don't mind—but we have to postpone our trip to town under the circumstances."

"I understand. I'll help you finish today and we can go to town tomorrow."

Tanya couldn't help but smile at the irony. She'd seized the idea of staying here today in hopes he'd go on to town without her and she'd be spared the constant vigilance she had to maintain against his magnetic aura.

Instead, she would be trapped with him in the kitchen all day. "I can manage," she said. "Really."

"I don't mind."

"I know, but—"

His grin, white and swift, flashed on his face again. "Ah—my extreme handsomeness is making you nervous again, hmm?"

From anyone else, Tanya might have resented his pseudoarrogant teasing, but it was impossible to mind it from Ramón. For one thing, he really was devastatingly handsome. For another, she liked the idea of him defusing the tension between them like that. With a mocking smile, she said, "You've caught me again."

"I'd try to be as ugly as the chili man, but you know it's hard to hide a face like this."

Tanya laughed. "It must tough. I feel for you."

He flung up his hands in mock despair. "You have no idea!" From a basket hanging near the stove, he took four onions, two in each large hand, and put them on the counter. "I go to the store and the poor girls at the registers can't even get the numbers right. Little girls giggle behind their hands."

Following his lead, Tanya opened the freezer and took out two trays of cold, roasted chilies. She put them on the table next to a glass bowl. She flashed him a smile. "The trials and tribulations of being the most handsome man in the land."

He inclined his head and gave her a wink. Raising his chin toward the trays of chili, he asked, "What are you doing? Are you freezing them with the skins on?"

"No. If you chill them for a while, the skins come off more easily—and you don't get blisters. I had blisters so bad once that I couldn't do anything for two days."

"Me, too." He began to peel the onions deftly.

Tanya settled at the table to start skinning chilies. Under her breath, she hummed "Amazing Grace," which had been planted in her mind by Desmary's comment. Ramón didn't seem to mind it. He peeled and chopped onions, and peeked into the oven several times to shake a tray of chilies. It was very companionable.

When he finished chopping onions, he left them in a neat pile on the counter and sat down with Tanya. "So, how is it going, anyway? Are you settling in okay?"

She smiled. "Sure. I've never had a bedroom like that in my life. It's like living in a fancy hotel."

"I always liked that room," he said. "It seemed like it would fit you. Of course, I had no idea how much you'd changed."

"It still suits me, though."

"Maybe." He lifted a shoulder. "After seeing you, I might have left it a little simpler."

"I'm glad you didn't," Tanya said. "I really missed pretty things like that."

"Yeah, you were a real girly girl back in the old days. You even had a bow in your hair."

"Not fair—I was a bridesmaid. Bridesmaids always have to wear ridiculous dresses and silly bows and dyed pink shoes." She rolled her eyes. "Ick."

Adroitly he skimmed a skin from the body of a chili and put the limp and naked flesh into the bowl with the others. One black brow lifted. "I seem to remember the dress was just fine."

"It was purple lace!" Tanya remembered her dismay over the dress, and that morning, had fretted about the fit. Her breasts and tummy had been swollen with pregnancy. They'd cut the dress a little wide to start with, knowing she was pregnant, but it was still tight when she put it on.

"All I remember is the way it fit you."

"That was all Victor saw, too. He wasn't going to let me be in the wedding at all."

"I'm sorry, Tanya, if you don't want to remember some of these things—"

"Don't apologize." To her amazement, Tanya had to physically halt herself from putting her hand on his arm. She had not voluntarily touched anyone in a long, long time. For a split second, she looked at the place where her finger had nearly lit—a smooth dark expanse of elegant skin, almost hairless and threaded with a sexy river of vein.

"I sometimes forget," he said, "that the day was so bad in the end."

Tanya nodded. "Me, too," she said, smiling. "Isn't that weird? That was probably the worst beating he ever gave me, but what I remember is talking with you for so long."

He said nothing, but his fathomless, milk-chocolate eyes were fixed on her face, waiting.

"You talked about Peru," she said, plucking another chili from the bowl.

"Did I?" he said, smiling. "I was planning my trip at that time."

Tanya felt the doors of memory creak open. Ramón then had been very thin—he'd probably not quite finished his growing, after all, and he was a lean man now. His glasses had made his eyes owlish and

obscured the lines of his face that she could see now—
the high cheekbones and clean jaw.

Her gaze flickered over his mouth—that impossibly sensual mouth. She still didn't quite understand
how she'd missed seeing how sexy his mouth was,
even at an inexperienced eighteen. A dangerous rip-
ple of longing moved through her body.

Hastily, she jumped up to check on the chilies in the
oven. "Did you ever go?"

"To Peru? Yes."

Tanya took out the cooked peppers and set them on
the counter. They sighed, as if exhausted, and she
glanced up to see if Ramón noticed. She found his
gaze on her body, lingering with appreciation on the
curves of breasts and hips. It was a delicious sensation, and with a cocky little smile, she put a hand on
her hip. "I have the same trouble you do," she said,
flicking an imaginary crumb from her shirt. "Everywhere I go, men fall at my feet."

He met her gaze, and now there was only the
smallest hint of a smile lurking at the edges of his
mouth. The dark eyes in their fringe of black starry
lashes were steady and secretive and inviting. As if to
drive his point home, he let his gaze drop to her lips.
"I would fall at your feet," he said, "but I can think
of better places to land." The smile broke free.

Tanya flicked him with a dish towel. "Behave," she
said and loaded another batch of chilies into the oven.

"I'll do my best."

But as she sat back down at the table, Tanya wondered if that was the kind of best she wanted. What was his other best? How could she bear to find out? How could she bear not to?

Resolutely, she said, "Tell me about Peru."

Chapter Five

Dear Antonio,
You don't realize what you'll miss until you don't have it anymore. I miss fall evenings, when the air smells like frost, and there are the sounds of wind in the leaves. And you pull your sweater close around you deliciously, even though it isn't cold enough yet for a coat, and it's only the anticipation that makes you shiver. I miss the way the stars look on such crisp apple nights, and the way home feels so cozy when you go back inside.

I used to read to you on those crisp nights. I

hope Ramón reads to you all the time. It's so important. But I think he knows that.

Be good, Antonito.

Love, Mom

They peeled and chopped chilies all afternoon, just Ramón and Tanya. As the hours passed, the day grew dark, and a storm threatened over the mountains. Lightning flashed and thunder rolled, but it was distant and untroublesome. Soon the yellow school bus would come down the road and stop at the narrow path which the boys' feet had made through the fields, and a tumble of young blue-jeaned, flannel-shirted bodies would pour out.

It made her feel very cozy to think of it.

"So," Tanya said into a lull. "We started to talk about Peru, but all you said was that you got to go. Why did you want to go there?"

"I don't know," he said slowly. "I can't really remember anymore. I think there was a film in school or something and I liked the way the mountains looked." He gave her a rueful look. "I didn't like Anglos very much and I liked the thought of going to a place where I'd be a part of the majority."

Tanya looked at him. "And was it what you thought?"

"No. It was more and it was less, but no place is ever really what you think it is."

"What was more?"

"The land. It's almost impossible to tell you how beautiful it is there. The mountains and the people and the customs—I loved it. I loved hearing Spanish being spoken all the time, too. Like a lot of children around here at that time, I spoke Spanish before I spoke English."

"And what was less?"

He smiled, and she liked the way small sun lines crinkled around the edges of his eyes. They were living lines, evidence of his maturity and his time on the planet. "I was still an outsider."

Tanya nodded. "Odd man out. I know that feeling." She paused, then found herself saying, "One of the things I liked about Victor was the way he made me belong to him. I wasn't on the outside anymore. If he could have inhaled me, he would have. It sounds weird, in light of what happened later, but he really made me feel safe."

"It doesn't sound weird." His hand moved on the table, as if he would touch her, then stilled. "It's like me and Peru. Same thing. We just needed different kinds of safety."

She gave him a sardonic little grin. "Some safety, huh?"

He acknowledged her irony with a quick lift of his brows. Beyond the kitchen, they could hear the sound of boys coming in from school, the uncertain tenors and altos mixing with the more certain bass of the older boys. Laughter and jests punctured the air as the boys shuffled toward the dining room to read the chores list and pick up the snacks waiting on the sideboard—cinnamon rolls and raisins this afternoon.

One of the counselors stuck his head into the kitchen. "Ramón, can I see you in here?"

"Be right there." He stood up and washed his hands. "Are you all right for dinner? Shall I send some more help?"

"I'll be fine," she said. "You've been a big help already. Thanks."

He winked. "My pleasure."

At the door to the dining room, he paused. "Tomorrow, barring bad weather, we're slated to harvest apples, so what about Monday for our trip to the library?"

"Fine."

"Have you ever harvested apples?"

Tanya shook her head. "Can't say that I have."

"You might like it. Why don't you plan to come with us down to the orchards."

"Great." Several boys had filtered into the room, dropping book bags in the usual corner before putting on aprons. Tanya lifted her chin to Ramón, and he left.

The boys who had drawn KP today ranged in age from ten to sixteen. Tonio was not with them, she noted with a little sense of disappointment. Sometimes he stayed in town to visit his girlfriend or go to debate practice. A van from the ranch would pick him

up just before supper, along with athletes and others
who had to stay at school for one reason or another.

One boy who did show up made Tanya considerably less happy, particularly since Desmary wasn't
here. At fifteen, Edwin Salazar was not the oldest boy
at the ranch, but he was the biggest, both in terms of
size and height. He had a brilliantly handsome face
and shiny ebony hair combed straight back from his
forehead. His eyes were beautiful and mean. A three-
inch scar marred his cheek.

He also knew he made Tanya nervous. Coming into
the kitchen today, he met her gaze with that almost
invisible, insolent smirk. "Hey, teach."

"Hi, boys," she said, wiping her hands on a towel.
The timer dinged and she bent to look at the chilies in
the oven. In the bald light of the oven bulb, they
swelled and shivered, and she had to smile. How had
she avoided noticing their breathing before this?

Behind her, the boys snickered at something Edwin said. She realized she was bent over in a rather
provocative position. But just how else would she get
the chilies out of the oven? A tight knot of fear tied
itself in her chest. This was the kind of dilemma Victor had made impossible. He would become insanely
jealous if a man looked at her—and woe be to Tanya
if she had encouraged him. But bending over? In a
work environment?

She breathed in the strong scent of chilies for a
moment. Edwin, speaking in Spanish, made a filthy
comment about her. A spark of old anger, ignited by

the wind of self-respect, burst into flame. Very, very slowly, she straightened. And turned.

In prison she had learned the best way to deal with the inevitable bullies and bosses was to meet them head-on. The more you ducked, the more they singled you out. You had to stand up to bullies—and that's all Edwin was, a big bully who'd never been taught any manners.

Narrowing her eyes, she simply stared at him for a moment. His little friend, standing alongside, snickered, and Edwin lifted his chin. He didn't speak.

Tanya said, "Bad language is against the rules here. Did you think it didn't count in Spanish?"

"How was I supposed to know you understood it?"

"Maybe you should assume people can always understand you."

Again the little friend snickered. Tanya cocked her head at him. "Disrespectfulness is also against the rules. Go. Tell the dorm master you have to have another chore today."

The smallest flash of triumph crossed Edwin's face. He started toward the door. "Not you, Edwin," she said. "Your friend. What's your name?"

The youth lifted his chin. "Mike."

"Mike, you're dismissed."

"Why? What did I—"

"Go."

He didn't argue anymore, but she could tell he was angry. So be it.

The other boys hung back, pretending to get started on the dishes, but she could see them watching how she would handle this big, mean boy.

She didn't know. She didn't want to make a mistake, ruin whatever chance he had to make his life better here. But especially in light of the harshly sexual aspect his comments took, she couldn't let him think he was getting away with something, either.

The beautiful mean eyes glittered. Fear touched her and just the faintest wisp of memory... Victor making that panting animal sound in his throat when he was going to beat her severely.

The memory lent her insight. She reacted strongly to this boy because he reminded her in some way of Victor. Fair enough—as long as she knew it, she could make decisions with clarity.

She willed herself not to cross her arms. He stood still as a sword, returning her gaze implacably. "C'mon, teach," he said. "What do you want me to do?"

Trust your instincts, a little voice told her. If she sent him away, he'd get what he wanted—out of KP. If she didn't, she'd have to deal with him here for more than two hours.

In a split second, she chose. "Wash your hands. You can peel chilies. Another word and you'll be in the kitchen every day for the rest of your stay here."

"You can't do that."

"Try me."

His eyes flashed, but he turned the water on in the sink, washed his hands, then flung himself down at the table. Tanya put a new bowl of roasted chilies on the table. Then she leaned close. "Let me tell you something. Where I've been, they eat babies like you for a late-night snack. Mind your manners with me. Is that clear?"

Without Edwin lifting his eyes, Tanya couldn't tell what expression they held, but he said in a voice seemly devoid of emotion, "Yes, ma'am."

The battle was over, Tanya thought, an old blues song running through her mind. The war would continue.

But today she had fought well.

Desmary was still tired at dinnertime, and took supper on a tray in her room. Tanya sat with her for a little while, listening to stories of the ranch in the old days as Desmary drank an herb tea the *curandera* in the hills above Manzanares had prepared for her.

When she was finished with the tea, she said, "Go on, child. I'll be fine in the morning. A battery this old just needs some recharging from time to time."

Tanya laughed. Collecting the dishes, she said, "You'll call me if you need anything, right?"

"Sure." She wiggled into her pillows more fully. "Thanks for your help with the chilies, Annie."

Tanya froze, her hands gripped tightly on the tray. Annie. The name carried painful associations with the past. "What did you call me?"

"You don't like it? It suits you, you know."

"No, I don't." She leaned on the door. "How does it suit me?"

"Annie is softer. Tanya just isn't the right name for you."

She swallowed. "I appreciate what you're saying, but please don't call me that anymore. It brings back bad memories."

"Put those dishes down and come here."

Tanya reluctantly did as she was told. Desmary took one smooth hand into her gnarled grip. "Don't let the past hold you. Not even a tiny piece of it, you understand?"

"You don't understand, Desmary, that name—"

"Oh, I understand all right. I remember Annie Quezada and how they clucked their tongues over her being in the hospital."

"How did you know?"

"I've been around forever, child. Back then, Ramón's mother lived here, taking care of her father. We gossiped like old women will about our children and nieces and nephews and dead husbands. She used to worry about you."

"I don't really remember meeting her."

"It's hard when you don't come from such a big family, to keep everyone straight. She met you several times, though, at family things. Victor was the child she worried about even when he was little. He stayed at the ranch sometimes when they were all children. He was mean, Annie. Mean to the bone.

And jealous of every scrap of attention anyone else ever got."

The soft conversation brought too many things bubbling to the top of the steaming caldron of memory. "I really don't like to think about these things any more," she breathed. She thought of Edwin in the kitchen this afternoon, his beautiful eyes hard, and knew that many adults had probably seen the same thing in Victor's eyes.

And yet—

"I really loved him, you know," she said to Desmary. "A lot of people don't understand that. But I did."

"I know you did, child."

"If there had been any other way to free Antonio and me from him, I would have taken it. I tried."

Desmary stroked her hand, slowly, and the gesture was deeply comforting. "I know."

Tanya looked down. "Every time I hear of some woman being gunned down in a parking lot, or at work, I'm so thankful that didn't happen to me."

To her amazement, Tanya felt tears streaming over her face. Tears of relief. Tears of anger—outrage for all those girls and women who still lived with that paralyzing terror. "You know what's evil? When I hear those stories, I get so angry I want to get a gun and kill all of those men who think they can love you to death."

"That's not the way, Annie. Violence begets violence."

"I know." She nodded, bowing her head against her arm, which was still stretched to meet Desmary's hand. How could it still hurt so much after so many years? How could there still be tears inside of her? "I know. I know it does."

Slowly the papery thumb moved on Tanya's knuckles. "You need to know that when Ramón brought Tonio here, he didn't speak for almost a year. We worried for a while that he'd been beaten, too. That he would be retarded."

Tanya frowned, sniffing. "He was talking pretty well by then."

Desmary nodded. "It hurt him, losing you. He didn't understand. One day, I was making cookies with him, and he just looked up and said, 'Mamma's dead.'"

Tanya looked down.

"I told him you'd just gone away for a long time. He would see you again one day. 'No,' he said. 'Mamma's gone.'"

"I don't know why you're telling me this."

"For one thing, you get as old as me, you know you could go in the blink of an eye." Desmary pursed her lips. "And if somebody doesn't give you some little pushes here and there, Annie, you're gonna live on the very edge of your life, scared to live, forever. That would be a shame."

Tanya nodded. It was true. She was afraid of everything. Except survival. Surviving she knew.

"Tonio never talked about you. Ramón brought you up sometimes, just to keep you in his mind. Tonio just ignored him. He never wanted to talk about it at all. When he was ten, Ramón sat him down and made him listen to the story of what really happened to you. It didn't help. Tonio still felt unwanted."

An ache burned in Tanya's chest. "I wanted him safe."

"One day, he'll understand that." Desmary's rheumy eyes were compassionate. "First, he needs to remember his mama, the one he loved. Her name was Annie. That's what I'm going to call you."

Surprised, Tanya smiled. "All that for one declaration?"

Desmary chuckled. "I'm an old woman. I'm allowed to take my time rambling around the point of my stories."

"I guess you are." Tanya kissed her forehead. "Thank you. My own mother was always too afraid of my father to be much of a comfort to me." At the look on Desmary's face, Tanya hastened to add, "Oh, he wasn't physically abusive—he was just a jerk."

"Ah." She slapped Tanya's thigh. "Go on out there now. Grab on to your new life and start living it."

"I'll try."

* * *

Ramón was a little late coming in to dinner. He found Tonio and Tanya already seated. "Sorry. I got caught up," he said, sitting down.

Tonio shrugged. Tanya stood to ladle stew into his bowl. "No," he said, "I'll serve myself. You eat."

"I don't mind," she said simply, and filled the bowl, then gave him a napkin-lined basket of rolls. Their hands brushed on the basket. Silly as it was, Ramón thought he felt a charge of something—it startled and pleased him. He looked at Tanya. She simply smoothed her hair back from her face and sat down.

He was an idiot.

Spreading margarine on the roll, Ramón looked at his son. "How was school? Did you get that report done on time?"

Tonio scowled. "Why do we have to talk about school every time? Don't you have anything else you want to talk about?"

Ramón frowned. "Sure—after you tell me about school. Is there something wrong?"

"No." Tonio's utterly sullen teenage scowl darkened. "I just want to talk about something else. Is that a crime?"

From the corner of his eye, Ramón saw Tanya lower her head and cover her mouth. For a minute he thought she was upset, then he caught her eye and saw the dancing light in the dark blue irises. Her nostrils flared dangerously.

Ramón looked away hastily, afraid her amusement would trigger his own and they'd both laugh, making a vulnerable teenager feel even worse. "We don't have to talk about school then." He wondered if the annoyance had to do with the report he had mentioned. "How is your girlfriend—Teresa?"

"I don't have a girlfriend," he said. "She's going out with Edwin Salazar now."

Tanya's head came up. Ramón saw the wary coyote expression cross her face—alert and skittish. He frowned. Edwin was the worst case they had at the ranch, and there had been a lot of debate over whether to let him come in. In the end, Ramón had voted to allow him at the recommendation of a social worker he trusted. Edwin had been abused by not only his father, but also other relatives, and the social worker hoped that Edwin had a chance at rehabilitation if he could see a normal environment. Ramón made a mental note to ask Tanya about the boy, but in the meantime, he had a wounded child. "I'm sorry, son," he said.

Tonio shrugged, his face thunderous.

"That doesn't help much, does it?"

"No." He lifted his eyes. "I want to know how to get her back."

Ramón took a breath. "Is that what you really want? She's chosen someone else—that means her feelings aren't the same as yours, right?"

"I guess."

"So wouldn't it be more satisfying in the long run to let her go and find somebody who likes you as much as you like her?"

Tonio's lip curled. "Jeez, Dad, do you think you could be any more wise?"

Ramón glanced at Tanya. "You're a female," he said. "Tell him what you think."

The wariness had made a mask of invisibility over her features. Her mouth was without expression, her eyes opaque as if there was nothing at all behind them. A single wisp of streaked hair hung next her cheek. Her gaze slid from Ramón's to Tonio's. "I think there's nothing that will make it better except time. And nothing we say will make it hurt any less. Just let it hurt and go on."

Tonio stared at her for a long minute, then abruptly, he stood up and left the table. Ramón started to go after him for his lack of manners, but Tanya stood with him and touched his arm. She shook her head. "He doesn't want to cry in front of us."

Her nearness slammed into him. She was so much smaller than he—her head just came to his shoulder—and her body was lean on a frame of surprising strength. Her hand was on his upper arm and he could feel the press of her fingers against his muscle like four small round brands.

Slowly, he looked at her, looked down into her piquant face and thought again of the Madonna in his old parish church. As he looked into her eyes, the opaque shield fragmented, and he saw the heat below. She wanted him, too. While he was thinking of her mouth, she was thinking of his. While he imagined lifting his hand to gauge the weight of her breasts against his palm, she was thinking of his chest and what it would be like bared. He wanted to offer a trade, but she was still far too skittish.

Instead, he just looked at her, and let the heat of their close bodies mingle, let his gaze touch her mouth and her neck, let her fingers move on his arm ever so tentatively. He let his desire show. And waited for her to run away.

For a long time, she didn't. She just looked up at him with that stricken expression, her fingers lingering on his arm. He didn't move.

At last she looked at her hand on his arm and removed it. "That's twice today I've touched someone willingly," she said. "I don't do that."

He winked. "I'm irresistible."

In gratitude, she smiled. "Let's eat, O Magnificent One," she said. "My eyes are well fed, but my stomach still needs some filling."

For an instant, he wondered if he could make her forget her stomach. He wanted to try. Instead, he sat down and put his napkin in his lap.

After dinner, they played chess and told jokes. And it wasn't until he was turning out his light many hours later that he realized he'd forgotten to ask her about Edwin.

Chapter Six

Dear Antonio,

The leaves are falling again—another cycle passing. I sometimes watch the wind blow across the desert and wonder what you're doing. Third grade now. You're probably a pretty big boy. My friend Naomi's boy was in to visit her last week, and I saw him. He was up to her chin.

Sometimes, now, I get so angry. For a long time, I didn't feel anything at all. But now I get so mad at the unfairness of all of this that I can't breathe. I just want to see you. For five minutes. I wouldn't even have to talk to you. I could just see you walk by.

I get angry at Victor's sisters for pushing to keep you away from me. I'm angry with myself for agreeing to a legal adoption. I thought it was the right thing, but I don't think it is anymore. I just want to see you. It hurts like a wound.

There's nothing to be done about it now. I guess I can hope to get out of here and see you. They're moving me to medium security next week. It's a step in the right direction.

Love, Mom

The weather Saturday morning was overcast and cool, perfect for picking apples, Desmary told Tanya, who felt a little thrill of anticipation at the coming activities. She wore her new blue sweatshirt and her good running shoes and a pair of jeans, her hair pulled back in a barrette. With good cheer, she put on a pair of silver feather earrings and took pleasure in the swing of them against her neck.

Tonio came into the kitchen as Tanya was mixing a second batch of pancakes. The flesh around his eyes was a little swollen, as if he'd slept very hard. For the first time, Tanya glimpsed the little boy he'd been, and her heart pinched a little. "Hi," she said with a small smile.

"Hi." He stepped close to her. He was taller than she by three or four inches and she looked up, taking deep pleasure in the arrangement of his features, the blueness of his eyes, the blackness of his hair. Such a handsome young man.

"You mind if I give you a hug?" he asked.

Startled, she said, "No, not at all."

He bent and awkwardly put his arms around her shoulders, elbows sticking out, the rest of his body held away from her. It was clumsy and self-conscious, but for one hard, strong minute, Tanya touched the shoulder of her son and smelled the soap on his skin and the shampoo in his hair. It was so sudden and sharply pleasant she couldn't breathe.

"Thanks for what you said last night," he said, and straightened, ducking his head as if he were embarrassed. "It helped a lot."

"I'm glad."

He shoved his hands in the pockets of his baggy jeans and shuffled backward. "I just wanted to tell you."

She smiled and nodded. "I'll send out pancakes for you and your dad in a few minutes."

When he had exited, Tanya looked at Desmary, and took a huge, clearing breath.

Desmary smiled.

Tanya shook her head, and went back to ladling pancake batter onto the grill. She couldn't think about it yet, or she'd cry.

After breakfast about twenty boys, including Tonio and Edwin, who cut each other a wide berth, along with two counselors, and Ramón and Tanya gathered outside in a little square of bare earth made by the house, the barn, the corrals and the dorms. A faint misty rain fell, hardly noticeable except for the jackets they needed to keep warm. Big stacks of bushel baskets waited by the barns.

"Listen up, everybody," Ramón said. "Some of you have been here long enough that you've done this before, and I expect you to help the others who haven't."

A voice at her elbow said, "Have you done it before?"

Tanya looked down and saw Zach standing there. The sleeves of his jean jacket were too short, the cuffs frayed, and he wore only a thin T-shirt underneath. She frowned and knelt without thinking to button his jacket. "Don't you have another coat?" she whispered.

"I'm all right."

"Okay." She stood up again to listen to Ramón explain the process of harvesting the apples. Next to her, a slim cold hand slipped into her own. She curled her fingers around Zach's hand.

The counselors passed out small canvas bags that could be slung around the shoulder. Ramón illustrated how to wear them.

"Now you all get to climb trees, but do it carefully. If you break branches, we don't get fruit from that branch next year. If you don't want to eat a bunch of bruised, disgusting apples, you also have to put them carefully into your bag, and carefully into the bushel baskets. You'll be the ones to suffer, all

right?'' He pointed to the baskets. "Everybody grab
some baskets and let's get this done."

The group headed down the dirt road toward the
small orchard. About thirty trees stood in neat rows,
the grass below their branches thick and green, unlike the rest of the prairie surrounding it. A narrow
irrigation ditch snaked around it.

Ramón dropped back. This morning, he wore his
usual jeans and jacket, with tennis shoes instead of
boots. Tanya found the change oddly sexy. "Do you
think you know what to do?" he asked.

"Sure. Lift, don't yank, and don't drop them,
place them in the bags."

"If you don't feel like getting up on a ladder, you
can be in charge of seeing that the bags get emptied
properly."

"No way. I haven't been in a tree in a long time."

Ramón looked at Zach. "Will you look out for her
for me?"

Solemnly, Zach nodded.

For hours they picked apples, shinnying up and
down the orchard trees. Tanya, hanging on a branch
below Zach, who was far too much of a daredevil for
her tastes, listened to the sounds of the boys. Chatter
and laughter punctuated with the peculiarly Latin-
Indian "ahhh" that was like "gotcha" in English.

Toward noon, there was a stir at one end of the orchard—shouts and the dismayed cry of other boys
trying to prevent a fight. A tumble of boys rushed by

below her. Over her head, Zach cried out, "Look! Tonio and Edwin!" He started to scramble down.

And slipped.

Tanya saw him lose his grip. Instinctively, she reached for him, managing to catch hold of the fabric of his jean jacket. The force of his falling body yanked her loose and she tumbled off the branch behind him.

It wasn't far, but her position was awkward and she was afraid of landing on Zach and hurting him. With a twisting reach, she flung herself clear, but the heel of her right hand struck the ground first and took all of her weight. A sharp, stabbing pain sliced her arm. With a small cry, she rolled and got to her feet, clasping her arm to her chest.

"Zach! Are you all right?"

He was on his knees, coughing, and Tanya bent over him. "Are you okay? Did anything get hurt?"

"No." He put a hand to his chest. "Just got the wind knocked out of me."

She patted his back. "That was quite a fall."

"Scared me."

"Are you okay?" Her arm stung sharply and she looked down. Blood spilled from a long jagged cut in the soft flesh of her forearm.

"You're cut!" Zach cried.

Tanya shrugged out of her jacket and wrapped it tightly around her arm to stanch the blood. A fine trembling stirred in her limbs, the first signs of shock. She looked for Ramón. The cut would need stitches.

A spate of furious Spanish curse words blued the air. Tanya and Zach whirled. A burly counselor held a struggling, yelling Tonio against his chest. Blood marred the boy's lip. Edwin stood off to one side, breathing hard. The bandanna he wore to hold his hair from his face had fallen off, and thick hair washed onto his forehead. Tanya felt chilled at the expression on his face.

A second counselor picked Edwin's bandanna from the grass and gave it to him. Edwin took it without a word, his flat gaze fixed on the counselor dragging Tonio away.

Ramón materialized beside Tanya and Zach. "I saw you fall. Are you okay?"

Finally Tanya lifted her arm and peeled back the jacket. Blood soaked the fabric. "No," she said. "Sorry. I need some stitches."

Ramón winced and reached for her. "Oh, *pobrecita.*" Lightly, he took her elbow in his fingers and pulled her closer. "You're right." He tugged the jacket back around her arm. "Keep it tight, and let's get you to town."

Tanya swallowed. She licked her top lip and tasted salt. "It won't hurt much till later," she said, and heard the breathy sound of it.

She felt Ramón's gaze sharpen. "Zach, run and tell Mr. Mahaney what I'm doing, okay? Tell him he's in charge until I get back. Can you do that?"

Wide-eyed, Zach nodded. "Sorry, Ms. Bishop. It's my fault."

"Oh, no, honey, not at all!" She bent and touched his head. "I wasn't paying attention and I slipped, that's all."

The boy's mouth tightened, and Tanya knew he still felt guilty. Dull pain throbbed along her arm, and she sucked in a breath. She would deal with Zach's feelings later. To Ramón, she said, "Let's stop and get some ice at the house. That will help."

"Can you make it to the house, or do you want me to go get the truck?"

"I can walk."

"Let's go."

It was not the most fun she'd ever had, Tanya had to admit. As hard as she tried to keep her arm still, there was no way to keep her movements fluid enough so that the arm wasn't jarred at all.

But it was oddly warming to have Ramón with her. At the house, he made her sit on the porch while he went inside. A few minutes later, he returned with a plastic bag of crushed ice and a towel.

Kneeling in front of her, he made a table of his knees and spread the towel over it. On the towel he put the large bag of crushed ice and smoothed it until it was a squat, wide shape. Gently, cupping her elbow and lifting the arm with one flat finger below the straight bone, he settled her arm in the cradle of ice. The first touch burned like the devil and Tanya made a noise. Tears stung her eyes.

He covered her hand with his own and looked at her. "I'm sorry. I know it hurts."

Breathlessly, she said, "Have you had stitches?"

As if he recognized her need to shift her focus, he smiled. "Not a one, actually. It's pretty amazing, considering how much time I've spent with horses." Firmly, he wrapped the towel around and around her arm to hold the ice. "Broken bones, that's what I had. Twice on each wrist, three fingers, two toes, and—" he grinned ruefully, drawing a finger over his dented cheekbone "—my cousin broke my face."

It seemed sick to laugh about it, but Tanya did, anyway. "Yeah. Mine, too."

His liquid gaze softened. "What do you know—we have something in common."

"Broken faces?"

"Laughing in spite of broken faces."

Tanya bit her lip, a thick stirring in her chest. A light wind stirred his wavy hair, and a strand touched the small indentation below his eye. In the gray day, his skin seemed incredibly perfect—supple and smooth and golden. His gaze held hers steadily, and that was where the true beauty of him was, in those fathomless, unutterably kind eyes. The expression in them shifted as she stared at him, turned molten and rich, and Tanya found her gaze slipping to his mouth, then back up. "Laughing can save your mind," she said.

"Yes." He remained kneeling for a moment, then stood and held out a hand to her.

As she stood up, David Mahaney, the counselor who'd dragged Antonio away from the fight, came striding over the open square. "You'd better wait a minute and see if Tonio is okay," she said.

"Tonio is fine. Come on."

"Ramón!" David called. "What do you want me to do with Tonio?"

"Just treat him like you'd treat one of the others."

David scowled. "That's not fair, Ramón. He's a good kid."

"Yes, he is." A hard sinew marked his lean jaw. "I want him to stay that way. He goes to his room with no supper."

"You know what a creep Edwin is," David protested. "He probably took the kid's girlfriend just because she liked Tonio. He's been on Tonio since he got here."

Tanya's arm throbbed, and her heart ached. A cool wind touched her face. She wanted to cry for all of them—Tonio and Ramón and even Edwin, who was far, far too young to be so hard.

"Violence solves nothing," Ramón said, opening the truck door. "Tonio has to learn that like everyone else. Now, if there's nothing else, this woman is bleeding like a stuck pig and needs stitches."

"You're making a mistake, Ramón." David put his hands on his hips. "I'm speaking as your friend. He's a good kid. Don't punish him for this."

A warm color washed over Ramón's cheekbones, and Tanya could see the mark where the bone had been broken under his right eye. "Back off," he said in a dangerous voice. "Being strict doesn't hurt kids. Being permissive hurts them."

"But—"

"A week of KP duty. That's as lenient as I'm willing to be." Ramón got in the truck and slammed the door. Tanya walked around and climbed in the other side. Without a word, he drove off toward town.

At the small clinic, Ramón waited in the front while Tanya was led back into the bowels of the place. He played with some toddlers and watched a young girl, enormously pregnant, fidget restlessly, swinging her foot back and forth. She couldn't have been more than sixteen. She should have been popping bubble gum while she doodled in the margins of her history notebook, not sitting in a clinic waiting for her baby to be born.

Looking at her pretty, ever-so-young face, he was reminded of the reasons he'd started the ranch in the first place—and he wished he could open another, for the girls who were his boys' counterpoints. Truth was, though, girls weren't often violent offenders, or even particularly criminal. Girls were arrested for shoplifting, boys for burglary. Girls were arrested for forgery, boys for armed robbery. Girls were arrested for disturbing the peace, boys for assault.

Not always, of course. He'd known some mean, bad girls in his time in the probation system. Hopeless. But girls turned their brutal anger inward. Boys turned it outward—and so boys got more help. Girls got pregnant. Hooked up with a bad guy. Ended up on welfare, or maybe even in prison, but no one noticed as long as it wasn't society toward whom the anger was directed. Boys took assault rifles into the streets.

The girl noticed his stare and turned a heavy-lidded gaze toward him, as if daring him to say a word. Her eyes were lined with thick eyeliner, black, her cheeks powdered white, her lips rouged a strong red. Her hair was meticulously styled, long and curly.

He ached for her, but forced himself to look away. Maybe one day, one of his boys would find her, and the manners and respect he'd learned would make him a good man for this girl. A man who would take care of the child she carried and make sure she didn't have to stand in a welfare line, a man who would love her. It was all he could do.

A doctor in a white coat came out of the back. "Ramón?" he said. "I need to talk to you."

Ramón got to his feet. John Arranda, the doctor, had been his friend since high school. He had a kind face and a goatee neatly trimmed, and warm dark eyes. "What's up?"

John touched his nose. "You know this woman?"

He nodded.

"I just got her X rays back." They had wanted an X ray because of the fall. "This arm has been broken in three places at different times." He held the gray-and-black negative up to the light, pointing with the eraser end of a pencil to one heavily scarred place just above the elbow. "This one didn't get much help for a while. It healed badly. It has to hurt pretty bad in the cold."

"She was abused when she was younger."

John lowered the film. "I see. Is she out of that situation now?"

"Yes." Ramón swallowed the rising anger in his throat and looked away. "Yes, she's away from it. Has been for a long time."

"Nobody breaks this part of their arm," John said quietly, touching the place above his elbow. "He probably hit her with something."

"Yes." Ramón took a long breath and blew it out.

John regarded him without speaking for another minute. "Come on in and hold her hand while I sew her up."

Ramón followed John into the examining room. Tanya lay on the table, her eyes closed. She looked pale, but otherwise okay. As John and Ramón came in, she opened her eyes. Seeing Ramón, she smiled.

Bright emotion stabbed him, and he went to stand alongside her. "Doc said I should come hold your hand. Is that okay with you?"

Wordless, she nodded. Ramón looked down at her slim small hand lying next to her thigh on the table. He picked it up and sandwiched it between both of his own. Her fingers were cold and he rubbed them between his palms, smiling. "Cold hands, warm heart."

Tanya smiled.

It aroused him. He couldn't help it. Her smile was as sweet and ripe as a chocolate-covered cherry, and he wanted to taste it. He wanted to mold his hands to her breasts, and open his palm on her belly. He wanted her.

Her fingers jumped against his palm. Ramón closed his eyes, and smoothed his palm over her fingers again, willing his desire back to wherever it lived. It didn't help a lot.

"Ready?" John asked.

Ramón looked at Tanya. She took a breath and nodded. John removed the cotton covering the wound and gave her a shot, then took out his needle. It took twelve stitches.

"Done," John said.

Tanya sighed hugely. "That wasn't so bad."

Ramón stroked her hand. "You've been so good, I'll buy you an ice cream when we're done here."

"Rocky Road?" The blue eyes glinted.

"Whatever you want, *grilla*." He restrained himself from touching her face. "Whatever you want."

"Careful, now," she said, and her grin turned impish. "You say 'whatever' and I might ask for a lot."

Ramón chuckled. "What you want, I've got."

Tanya looked at John. "He's terrible."

"Yes. Always has been." John finished cutting a tube of gauzy material and skimmed it over Tanya's arm. "You have to watch out for his type, you know."

Tanya looked at Ramón, and a curious sobriety touched the dark blue irises. "I know."

Chapter Seven

Dear Antonio,

I have met an amazing woman. Her name is Iris, and she is in prison for three life terms for crimes I'd rather not tell a boy. She's been in prison since she was nineteen, and she's quite a bit older than me—though I couldn't tell you for sure how old. Around here, you don't ask what people don't volunteer.

The thing is, she has given me keys to cope. I've been having very hard times the past six months. I've done all the educational things they have to offer, and I read all the time, but it isn't the same. You never forget you're in prison, that it isn't a normal place or way of being. You sometimes think it would be better to die and be free than stay here another day.

Iris has shown me how to live in the moment. In the very single moment there in front of me. To smell it and taste it and enjoy or endure whatever is in that moment. It sounds so simple a thing to make such a big difference, but I know it has saved my life.

Love, Mom

"So, you want Rocky Road, huh?" Ramón asked as they came out of the clinic. The earlier drizzle threatened to turn to real rain. Tanya watched Ramón turn the collar of his jacket upward.

"You don't have to buy me ice cream."

"I want to. It'll make me feel better." He reached for and clasped her free hand, then let it go, as if remembering she didn't like it.

The funny thing was, she was getting used to being touched again. Between Tonio, Zach and Ramón, there wasn't much chance someone wouldn't be touching her at one time or another.

"I'm hungrier than ice cream," he said. "Let's get a sandwich or something. If you're feeling okay."

"I'm really hungry," she said. "Any good hamburgers in town?"

He winked. "I know just the thing. C'mon." And he took her hand again. "Do you mind?" he added, lifting their joined hands to illustrate. His long brown fingers looked strong and graceful, and she liked the way his skin felt against her own. It felt like a big deal, holding hands. "I don't mind," she said quietly.

He took her to Yolanda's, a small, happy old-fashioned diner. The floors were wooden, the booths of dark red vinyl, and the tables had ranch theme tablecloths thrown over them, little Bar S and Half Moon brands on a brown plaid background.

They settled in a booth by the front window, and Tanya looked out at the gray day, feeling snug. A waitress offered coffee, and both of them accepted with enthusiasm. "And we want a couple of hamburgers, with fries," Ramón said. "Cheese on one. Tanya?"

"Please."

"You got it," the waitress replied, scribbling their order on a small green order pad. She picked up the laminated menus they hadn't examined and hurried away.

Gingerly, Tanya put her arm on the table and touched the bandages. "It's probably going to be a few days before I can lift anything," she said ruefully. "Good thing it wasn't my left arm—I'd hate to leave Desmary with all those apples to chop."

"Are you left-handed?"

"Yes."

"So is Tonio." He smiled. "I didn't even realize it until he started school. He eats with both hands."

Tanya inclined her head. "Is he creative, then?"

"Some. His real gifts are in the analytical realm, though. He loves numbers and formulas and engine parts."

"Victor did, too."

Ramón's dark eyes went opaque. "Tonio has a picture of his dad in front of that old Fury, which Victor restored. Remember the picture?"

"Yes. I took it."

The waitress brought thick ceramic mugs of coffee. Tanya stirred in sugar. "Does Tonio ever talk about Victor or me? Does he ever see the rest of family? Any of Victor's sisters?"

"No." Ramón sighed. "They used to come to visit when he was younger, but we haven't seen any of them in a long time."

A small crackle of anger rustled on her nerves. To smooth it, she breathed in slowly. "At one time, I really believed I had acted in Tonio's best interests by agreeing to the custody arrangements." She hadn't actually seen Ramón—he had conducted his business by letter. "Even then, I was wise enough to realize you had qualifications none of the rest of them did." She frowned. "What made you come forward, Ramón? I've never asked."

"No one else wanted to adopt him."

Stunned, Tanya stared at him. "What?"

"They didn't want him because he had your blood."

The anger crackling on her nerves grew more intense. "But rather than give me any joy at all, they pushed for me to give him up to you totally." As if the anger had clotted in the swollen pathways of her arm, a sudden pulse of pain struck her wrist. "Sometimes, Ramón, I look back and can't believe how foolish I was—how weak and malleable."

"No." His jaw was hard as he reached over and put a hand on hers. "You weren't weak. Not ever. You were young and without help and you did the best you could." His nostrils flared with strong emotion. "You stayed alive."

Tanya lifted her chin. "Yes, I did."

His eyes glittered with something she couldn't read but somehow it stirred her. The rustling on her nerves turned softer and warmer. Fluid awareness pooled in her breasts and washed over her thighs, and she found herself imagining how his body would feel against her own. As she stared, it seemed he knew her thoughts, for the hand that he had allowed to rest on hers shifted, and his long, graceful fingers moved in a light, erotic pattern over her inner wrist. "I'm glad," he said.

As if aware that the conversation had taken a deeply intimate turn, he leaned back suddenly and lifted his coffee cup in a toast, offering a smile in place of the heady sensuality on his face only moments before. "To life!"

Tanya lifted her cup. "To survival."

"Not survival," he said. "There's so much more to life than that, cricket."

For a moment, she only looked at him. She didn't want the rest—no passion, no wild highs and lows, no despair or great joy—just simple, calm day-to-day survival. "I didn't mean it in the grim sense."

The waitress appeared. "Here we go," she said, but hardly paused before bustling away again. She sailed by once more, dropping a bottle of ketchup and one of mustard on the table.

"Smell that," Ramón said and smiled at Tanya. "There's a lot to be said for simple pleasures."

Tanya piled everything—pickles, lettuce, tomatoes, onions, ketchup and mustard—onto the burger. Awkwardly with the bandages, she lifted it in both hands and took one second to savor the salty, rich scent before she bit into it. Juices exploded on her tongue—a perfect melding of salt and fat and crisp cold vegetables and pungent sauces. She closed her eyes, savoring the flavor.

"Little things are everything," she said when she could speak. "Everything."

Ramón only nodded, a strangely stricken expression on his face. "Eat your cheeseburger, Tanya. And then I'll show you a bookstore I think you'll like."

"Shouldn't we get back soon?"

"They'll manage without us."

She shrugged. "Okay."

By the time they emerged from the diner, the rain had stopped, but a cold wind had blown in behind it, sharp and piercing. The sky was still gray and heavy-looking. Tanya said, "It almost feels like snow."

He lifted his chin, smelling the air. "Maybe. I think it's a little ways off yet, but you never know. Last year, there was snow on the Sangre de Cristos by the end of August."

"That's early." Tanya huddled deeper into her coat. The mild tranquilizer she had finally accepted at the hospital, combined with the terrific hamburger, made her feel warm and calm.

As they walked down the largely deserted streets, Ramón told her about the owners of the bookstore. The man had fled his native Mexico as a young man. "I think," Ramón said with a smile, "that he was wanted by the law, but it has never been said in so many words."

"Ooh," Tanya said, "a desperado."

He nodded. "Someone wanted his skin. He ran into the mountains and fell ill. A very beautiful young woman found him and took him to her grandmother, who was a famous and powerful *curandera,* one of the local healers."

Tanya smiled. "And he fell in love with the young girl as the grandmother healed him."

"You've heard this story before." A glitter shone in his dark eyes.

"Variations, anyway."

"Ah, well, you know then, that the girl was as gifted as her grandmother, and became a *curandera,* too. He runs the bookstore, and she dispenses herbs and potions to everyone in town.''

''Very romantic.''

''You'll love the bookstore. You still like to read, don't you?''

She chuckled. ''Trust me—prison makes readers of non-readers. The ones who were readers to begin with turn into fanatics.''

''I can imagine.''

He stopped in front of an old building. A plate glass window had been painted with the words Walking Stick Bookstore in an arch. Below it read Cesaro Valdez, Proprietor. Across the bottom of the window were more gold letters: Knowledge is power.

''Nice,'' Tanya said.

''Are you sure you're feeling all right?'' Ramón asked, pausing outside.

''I'm fine.'' She looked at him. ''Later, I will be miserable. Tomorrow, I may be grouchy. By the day after tomorrow, life will be back to normal. Right now, I feel just fine.''

He laughed. ''Okay. I'll save my worrying for tonight.''

She gestured toward the door. ''Getting some good books to keep me company later might be just right.''

As she stepped into the store, Tanya instantly fell in love. A scent of books and dust and cinnamon tea struck her nostrils, and from hidden speakers played soft Andean flute music. A rabbit warren of bookshelves, illuminated with small lamps set alongside single chairs and small tables, stretched beyond her vision. She paused. Sighed.

A woman behind the counter smiled at them. "Ramónito!" she cried. "Where you been keeping yourself, *hijo?*" She came around the counter, a short, round woman with ebony hair swept with wings of white. She took Ramón's hands and looked him up and down. "You been working too hard again. I want to see some meat on those bones."

"Rosalia, this is my friend Tanya Bishop. She's cooking at the ranch with Desmary." He grinned devilishly. "Blame her for my skinniness."

Tanya grinned and rolled her eyes. Rosalia tsked. "Like I'd ever blame a woman for anything a man did!" A flicker moved in the almond-shaped eyes and she took her hands from Ramón and put them close to Tanya's bandaged arm. "May I?" she said.

Caught in the extraordinary depth of the beautiful eyes, Tanya nodded. The woman put both her palms on her arm, one just above the elbow, one just below. Tanya felt nothing, except the extraordinary warmth of Rosalia's fingers, but it was as if Rosalia were reading something, or listening. After a minute, she pursed her lips, then opened her palm and placed it, palm down against Tanya's. She looked at Ramón and jerked her head toward the books.

He made a noise of mock outrage, but smiled. "Okay?" he said to Tanya.

She nodded.

Rosalia stared into Tanya's face. "Tell me about the sorrow of this hand," she said, leading Tanya to a comfortable deep couch set behind the counter.

"I cut it on a stick. I felt out of a tree, just a little while ago."

Rosalia smiled. "No, not this new hurt, not that hand. Longer ago. Old wound." She covered Tanya's hand with her other one, making a warm sandwich, just as Ramon had done a little earlier. "There is damage here—if you don't heal it, there will be arthritis later."

Tanya tried to think of something she'd done to the hand, but could think of nothing. Perhaps she meant repetitive motion injuries, but Tanya cut with her left hand. "I don't know. Cooking?"

Slowly, the woman shook her head. Tanya became aware of the sound of pan flutes piped in quietly through speakers in the ceiling. Soothing and haunting. They increased the feeling of stepping into another time, another world. "No, cooking is a creative thing," Rosalia said. She frowned. "It's deep." She shook her head, rubbing her open palm in a circle over the bones of Tanya's hands.

Unbidden came an image of this very hand holding a gun up before her, and she knew that was the answer Rosalia sought. "I shot a man dead with this hand. A long time ago."

"Ah." Rosalia nodded, and slowly let Tanya go. "You go look at books."

Tanya backed away, sensing the woman was not dismissing her, but giving her room to come to terms with this new piece of self-knowledge. Iris, her friend in prison, had often done the same thing.

As she headed into the rabbit warren of bookshelves, Tanya kept her hands close to her belly, feeling bemused. The strange encounter might have been right out of "Twilight Zone," except Tanya had seen such women at work in the past. It was a gift, like any other. Like all nontraditional healers, *curanderas* relied on the harmony of body and mind and spirit.

And, too, there had been an odd thing about her right hand. For months after the shooting, she'd been unable to use it at all. It gave her terrible pain to even lift a glass of water. Repeatedly, prison doctors had examined it, but could find nothing wrong. A psychologist finally told her it was akin to hysterical blindness—when a person witnessed something too terrible to contemplate, they sometimes could not see. The hand that shot Victor carried the sorrow of the act for Tanya, who couldn't.

Moving her fingers, she remembered the terrible months just after the shooting. No one had understood how conflicted she'd been. They didn't understand that she had loved him once, that he'd fathered her child, that he could be a funny, loving man. He was evil, too, and that evil had caused his death as directly as Tanya's lifting the gun, but no evil came in the world without some hope. It was thinking about the good in him that upset her.

She twisted her mouth. Water under the bridge now, and she would not open the wounds again. Instead, she let the wonders of the bookstore seduce her, and wandered through the stacks. She saw Ramón in an aisle of music history. Tanya ambled toward the cookbooks and fell adrift in glossy pictures of French cottages, their tables overflowing with Provençal food.

She had no idea how long they were there, how long she spent drifting through one warren and into another. Outside, a second leg of the storm moved in, and mild thunder jumped in the heavens, lending the rooms an even cozier aspect. She carried two cookbooks, three paperback novels, and a Spanish-English colloquial dictionary. Although she'd spent several years reading and writing Spanish in prison—yet another of her endless self-improvement projects—she still got lost when the conversation moved very fast. It seemed everyone at the ranch could move between the two languages at will and she didn't like being at a disadvantage.

She came around a corner and found Ramón sitting on a sofa near a window. A tiny lamp burned on the antique table, and Ramón was washed gold with the incandescent bulb on the right, silver-gray from the window on his left. The fingers of light fanned over his high, clear brow, cascaded down his elegant cheekbones, danced on his generous, seductive mouth. Such a face, she thought, struck dumb once again.

He didn't seem to notice her, and Tanya clasped her books to her chest like a schoolgirl with a crush. Her lungs felt overfilled, her body too tender for the clothes she wore. Intelligence and compassion and a sense of humor—all showed in the exquisite features, along with the alluring seductiveness. How had he managed to avoid marriage all these years? How was it that some determined female had not corralled him by now?

At the diner earlier, Tanya had said she did not want life—but she did. She wanted to dance and make love, she wanted to cry out with passion and chortle with joy. She wanted to bear another child and have another husband and—

Be young and live.

She was afraid, too. Afraid of the intensity of her nature and the combustibility of Ramón's. He was genial, a generous man who would please almost any mother or matchmaker as a suitable husband candidate.

But Tanya was not the foolish sort of woman who mistook a kind man for a bland one. In his eyes was a fierce and blazing passion, carefully banked. He was a man who controlled himself rigidly and carefully, a man who kept his passions skillfully concealed, but she knew they were there. Waiting.

For her? She didn't know and didn't know if she wanted to find out.

A fleeting image of him, naked and close, gave her a momentary weak-kneed breathlessness. Embarrassed, she ducked her head and was about to turn away when he called her name in a loud whisper.

She turned.

"Come sit with me," he said quietly, gesturing. "I want to read you something."

On stiff legs, she moved toward him, creaking slowly down to perch on the very edge of the sofa next to him. "I only bite on Saturdays," he said.

Bite—oh, that brought up some images! She clasped the books closer to her chest. "It is Saturday."

"Ah, so it is." He waggled his eyebrows wickedly. "Well, I don't bite hard."

A shiver goosewalked down her spine. "Umm, what do you want to read to me?" Her voice sounded odd in her ears, all breathy and soft.

He put his book down next to him, on the cushion between them. Outside, thunder growled over the sky, and rain pattered musically at the windows. Inside, the haunting Andean flutes floated through the room. Within Tanya's chest beat a quick, fluttery pulse. It seemed impossible such tiny beats could circulate enough blood through her body, and as if to prove it, she felt a little light-headed.

Gently, he took her books from her arms and put them on top of his own, then shifted the pile to the floor at his feet. He moved closer. Tanya shrank away from him, overwhelmed with the narcotic scent of his skin, and the way the silver and gold light caught in the long strands of his dark wavy hair. Her heart beat faster, and to her dismay, she realized her hands were shaking. When he reached for her cheek with his fingers, she started violently, her gaze flying to his face.

He halted, then stretched out his hand again and lightly put his fingertips on her jaw. "I won't do anything you don't want me to do, *grillacita*, little cricket," he said, his fingers moving lightly. "But I really need to kiss you." His gaze touched her mouth, moved back to her eyes. "Will you let me kiss you, Tanya?"

She stared at him, wanting him and yet, so afraid. "Yes," she heard her voice whisper. And again, "Yes."

He opened his hand on her face, his fingers spreading to clasp her ear, his lean palm cupping her cheek. The touch was unbearably gentle, wildly arousing. To be touched at all was almost more than she could bear, and when he came closer, bending over to kiss her, Tanya panicked.

She put her hand up and stopped him, ducking her head away from him. "Ramón, no, I—it's just—this is—" Rising terror bolted through her and she started to stand up.

Ramón let her go instantly, but caught her good hand. "Hey. You don't have to run away."

Tanya swallowed, feeling faintly foolish as the panic attack eased. It was Ramón here, sitting next to her, his thigh resting against her own, looking so sensually handsome. Hesitantly, she lifted her hand to touch his face. He didn't move, just waited while she touched his jaw, his cheek, his chin. Beneath her fingers, his skin was warm and male, coarse where his light beard was shaved off his chin.

She looked where she touched, the fluttering pulse strong in her throat. He didn't move, and she was glad of his patience, glad of the heat and calm in his liquid eyes. "It scares me to want anything," she said.

"A kiss isn't such a big thing."

"Maybe not to you." She traced the clean, straight edge of his jaw. "It is to me."

Gently, slowly, he lifted a hand and smoothed hair from her face. "Not so much to win or lose, in a kiss."

Tanya raised her eyes to his infinitely dark, infinitely patient gaze. Suddenly she remembered sitting next to him at a card table covered with layers of blue, green and white tissue paper while a Spanish band sang a sad ballad she didn't understand, and wondering what it would be like to kiss him. The memory startled her—she must have repressed it, trying to remove any feeling of guilt she felt for that day.

Now, with small movements of her fingers, she urged him closer. Very slowly, he tilted his head and bent toward her. His breath, smelling faintly of the mint he'd eaten after lunch, brushed her face, warm and moist.

Their lips touched. His were full and firm, pliant and undemanding. Gently, he kissed her. Gently he moved ever so slightly closer, putting his hand under her hair. His thumb moved against her earlobe. She opened her eyes when he pulled back, and he met her gaze soberly, dipping to kiss her again. His hair curled around her fingers. His shoulder bumped her wrist.

It was only a dance of lips, a simple, warm exploration, and Tanya felt the terrible panic and tension leave her on a sigh.

Ramón straightened, his hand smoothing over her shoulder. "See, not so scary."

Tanya smiled at him, warmed clear through. "It was just your astonishing presence that scared me."

He laughed. "You made a joke."

"There's hope for me yet."

"Oh, there's always been hope for you, Tanya. Always."

Tanya looked toward the window, a pungent ache in her chest. There were two sides to every coin life passed. Victor had been the dark side; Ramón was the bright. "I'm so grateful to you, Ramón. I don't know how I would have survived all this without your help."

"Was that kiss one of gratitude, then?" he asked softly.

"I don't think so," she said. "I don't know."

"I don't think so, either." He took his hands from her shoulders and leaned over to pick up their books. He gave Tanya hers to carry. "We should get back to the ranch."

Tanya had the feeling she had disappointed him in some way, but she was not sure how.

No, that was a lie. It was dangerous to start lying to herself. She didn't have to share her feelings or observations, but she had to claim them, keep herself in touch with what she really felt. It was the only way to stay healthy and strong, able to cope with the changes her life had required.

Honesty. Clasping her books to her chest, she knew she had allowed Ramón to think she was expressing mere gratitude when she kissed him. Even more than allowing him to come to his own conclusions—she'd planted the idea.

It wasn't true, of course. Her wish to kiss him had nothing at all to do with gratitude and everything to do with desire.

He undoubtedly knew that. She rubbed her forehead. Maybe that was where the disappointment lay—in her lack of honesty. A vague, formless guilt tugged her. Maybe she shouldn't have allowed him to get so close. She shouldn't have allowed her emotions to show so blatantly on her face. Maybe—

Ramón stopped dead in the middle of a dark narrow aisle and turned around. With a suddenness that surprised her, he bent and pressed another kiss to her mouth. This time, his body touched hers, chest to chest, leg to leg. The kiss carried a strong edge of hunger. The insistent thrust of his tongue sent a sharp response through her middle.

"It wasn't gratitude, Tanya. A million years ago, we were attracted to each other and we still are." He put his forehead against hers and rubbed her jaw with his thumb. "It isn't wrong, and it also doesn't have to go anywhere."

She looked at him. "I don't know how to do that," she said.

"Do what?"

"Be lighthearted about things like kisses and feeling attracted to you."

He lifted his well-shaped head, and the devilish version of his devastating smile showed off his white teeth and made his eyes crinkle at the corners. He winked. "Stick with me, kid."

Tanya only smiled. She doubted anyone could teach her to lighten up, but if anyone could, it was Ramón.

Chapter Eight

Dear Antonio,

It's the small things that make you crazy. Like never going to the grocery store. I never liked it all that much, to tell you the truth, but right now it would be such a big pleasure to push a basket through the produce section and smell the onions and potatoes, see the pale green cabbages and dark kale and mottled butter lettuce, all piled up and dotted with silver water, reflected in the mirrors. I'd love to pick out peaches and put them in a bag to make a pound.

I'd love to examine packages of stew meat and pick out the best one, the one without too much fat. And I'd love to bring the groceries in and put them away on a stormy afternoon, knowing we were safe as I made tuna fish sandwiches and to-mato soup. Little things mean a lot, Antonio. If you can focus on the little things, the big ones won't hit you so hard.

Love, Mom

As they stepped out on the street, Tanya spied a Disabled American Veteran's store on the corner, and remembered Zach's ragged jacket. "Do we have time to stop in the DAV?" she asked.

"Money burning a hole in your pocket?"

Tanya realized he might not approve of her taking a personal interest in one of the boys. "I noticed this morning that Zach's jacket is too small. I'd like to see if I could find him another one. Would that be all right?"

"Yes. Very much so."

Inside, she made her way to the racks of boy's clothes and flipped through the coats. "He seems very young to be in the program," Tanya commented, tugging an army green surplus jacket off the rack. It was in good shape, but too small. She put it back.

"Zach?" Ramón took out a long black raincoat, and Tanya watched him put his hands on it, feeling it as he looked at it. "He was arrested sixteen times on petty theft and burglary. His mother kept him out of foster homes somehow or another, but she'd been doing drugs a long time, and died last spring." He put the raincoat back and pulled out a jean jacket to show Tanya, rubbing the sleeve between his fingers as if to gauge the weight. "This one?"

She examined it, found the elbows nearly bare and shook her head. "Poor Zach."

"He's pretty angry, and doesn't have a soul in the world on his side. It may be too late, but I had to try."

"And what about Edwin? What's his story."

Ramón scratched his eyebrow before he answered. "Attempted murder."

"And he's at the ranch?"

"We don't call it the Last Chance for nothing, Tanya. He's a hard case, but a lot of them are. Chris Lansky didn't attempt—he succeeded."

"He's only twelve!"

Ramón nodded. "There were extenuating circumstances, as they say, but all the same...." He shrugged.

Tanya pulled a dark blue jean jacket from the rack. It was the right size. "Edwin scares me," she said. "I try to be calm and cool, and I've handled him, but in my bones, I know he's dangerous."

"I noticed that you're uncomfortable when his name comes up." He flipped through several boy-size coats and without looking at her, pursed his lips. "Did you agree with David this morning, that I was too hard on Antonio?"

"No, not at all. You did the right thing—violence doesn't solve anything." The jean jacket was perfect.

Fully lined, without tears or badly worn places and a price tag in her range. "This will be perfect."

Ramón nodded. "David is a good counselor, but he doesn't always understand how hard some of these boys are. They've been living by the laws of the streets, which are life and death laws—'one false move and you're out' kind of laws. They have to be given the same hard laws on this side."

"Tonio hasn't lived that way."

"No." Ramón looked grim. "But he's always had a tendency to try violence first. A lot of boys do, but he's got a brooding side. I want to nip it in the bud."

"And he has to live by the same rules you've set for the other boys."

"Some, but there is a difference. He isn't in trouble—he's a member of my household, and therefore has more freedom."

They walked to the end of the aisle, and on wide shelves against the wall were dishes. Tanya paused to pick up a hand-painted china saucer, the edges rimmed with gold. The price tag was ten cents. "I used to collect these."

He took the saucer from her and turned it over. "Why?"

"I don't know." She grinned. "Does anyone have a reason to collect strange things?"

"Good point."

"They're unique and beautiful—and even when I've been very poor, they were in my price range. I can have ten for a dollar, right now."

"Or—" he bent and took a dinner plate that matched the saucer from a pile in the back "—you can have a matching set."

"Perfect."

For a moment, their eyes met, and a spark arced between them, gentle and powerful.

Ramón looked at his watch. "Desmary is going to kill us both if we don't get back pretty soon. Come on."

Tanya looked for Zach when she returned. From the foyer just inside the front door, she heard him in the kitchen, and leaving her purse on the table, headed down the hall. At the door, she paused. Zach sat at the table with Desmary and Tonio. The three of them sliced apples and dropped them in cold water for the cooking tomorrow. Dinner bubbled on the stove.

Tanya didn't realize how tired she was until she stood in the doorway. There she paused, feasting her eyes privately upon her child. He had a fat lip, the only evidence of his fight with Edwin, and his mood was considerably calmer than it had been earlier. Desmary directed with gestures more often than words. Zach, almost too small for the chair, swung his feet.

"You miss her?" Tonio was saying.

Zach nodded.

"Mad at her, too, though, huh?" There was a reedy quality to Tonio's voice, the cracked hollowness of adolescence. "What I remember about my mom is being mad."

Mothers. They were talking about mothers. Tanya shrank back, listening.

"Yeah," Zach said. "She didn't have to go and die."

"You don't know. Maybe she did." Tonio dropped a handful of apple slices into a bowl of water and grabbed another whole apple. "You gotta try and keep the good stuff."

"Is that what you did?"

"Yeah. As much as I could. I don't even have a picture of my mom—only one of my dad, so I don't remember what she looked like, but I can think of other stuff—like this perfume she used to wear, and pretty hair, really long and blond."

Tanya smiled. Her hair had never been particularly long. Children's perceptions were so different.

"But you know what I remember?" Tonio asked. "This weird song, about a lady who gets married the day before she dies."

"Eww."

"Sounds gross, but it was real pretty. She used to sing it to me before I went to sleep at night."

Raw pain sliced through Tanya's chest, and she backed out of the kitchen, unable to breathe. She ran smack into Ramón. He took one look at her face and said, "Come on, honey, let's get you to bed."

It had been too much of a day. Way too much. The fight in the orchard, her fall from the tree, the kiss from Ramón and now this. "I'm so tired."

She let him walk her to the door of her bedroom, then firmly stepped away. The bag she handed to him. "Give it to Zach, will you?"

"Why don't you just wait and give it to him to-morrow?"

Tanya nodded.

"Is there anything you need? Can I send someone up with some tea or something?"

"No," she said and looked over her shoulder. "No, I think I'm just going to go to sleep."

Ramón smiled. "Good. If you need anything, you know where to find me."

"Yes."

She bid him good-night and shut the door firmly—against him, against the painful memories the day had roused, against confronting the realities her new life offered. She kicked off her shoes, her bra and jeans, and fell into bed.

Ramón washed up and went down to dinner. Tonio, looking even more sullen than he had the night before, waited at the table with Desmary. To his surprise, Zach was there.

Ramón gave Desmary a questioning look. She lifted a comfortably padded grandmother shoulder. "He's little," she said.

For one moment, Ramón hesitated. He had to admit Zach tugged his protective instincts the same way the kid pulled on everyone else's. He was too young to have known so much trouble, and in spite of the problems he found at school and with other children, he possessed a basic sweetness of nature that made it hard to resist him. "All right," he said, and tension drained from Zach's body visibly, as if someone had pulled a plug on his big toe.

Touching his shoulder, Ramón said, "Napkin in your lap, guy. Elbows off the table.

"Do you have homework tonight?" he asked them both.

"I have math to do," Zach said. "Not much though."

"Are you good at math?"

Zach shook his head. "Not very. It's boring."

"What do you like?" Carefully, aware of the way Zach watched him, Ramón neatly cut his meat, put the knife down and shifted his fork to his right hand. "Music, maybe?"

"Music is for sissies." He cast a glance toward Tonio, who steadfastly ignored him. "I like art."

Ramón nodded. That didn't surprise him. "I bet you draw birds, don't you?"

"How'd you know that?"

"I've seen a few of them. You're quite an artist."

Zach shrugged. Ramón repeated the process of cutting his meat, then looked at Tonio. His plate of food was largely untouched. "Is your mouth bothering you?" Ramón asked.

Tonio gave him a sullen glance and shook his head.

"I couldn't quite hear you," Ramón said.

Tonio sighed gustily and said, "No."

"You need to eat something, then. Do you have homework tonight?"

"Yes."

Ramón grinned. "Shall I guess what it is? Do you have math like our little friend here?"

Not even a hint of a smile, Ramón noted with an inward chuckle. Often he could use a little teasing to bring healing to their relationship after a sharp punishment. He tried again. "English? Science?"

"Yeah and no." The faintest ease of features erased the scowl on Tonio's brow.

Ramón decided not to push it, but after supper, he called Tonio into his office. It was an old-fashioned room, with a long window facing the mountains. Shelves filled with Ramón's beloved books lined the walls—a good many of them in Spanish by the new wave of Latin novelists. It was one of the great joys of his life that he could read such beautiful novels in their original language.

Tonio draped himself over an overstuffed chair. He didn't speak, just sprawled, working a toothpick in his mouth, and waited for Ramón.

Ramón, too, took his time. He shelved several books, then sat down in the comfortable office chair he'd bought for himself two years ago. "We should talk about this, son. It isn't like you to be out of control."

"There's nothing to talk about."

"One of the things I've always liked about you, Tonio, is your strong feelings. But you can't let those feelings rule you. It's okay to be mad. Furious, even. It's okay to be frustrated and hurt and anything else." He leaned forward earnestly. "Feel anything you want to feel—it's all okay. You just can't act on those feelings inappropriately. And you have to eventually get to the moment when you ask yourself, what do I want?"

Tonio waited.

Ramón hated these scenes. Hated them and often wondered how much benefit they were. But he had them with almost all the kids, all the time. The boys were out of control, and had no disciplinary tactics to help themselves out of the sticky situations into which their mouths or hearts or screaming hormones got them.

He tried again. "What you really want doesn't have anything to do with Edwin."

"Oh, yes, it does. You know what I feel like when I see him? I want to break his face."

"Under the circumstances, that's a very normal feeling. It just isn't okay to do anything about it." Ramón clasped his hands. "The bottom line here is the girl. Teresa, right?"

Tonio nodded.

"Edwin could give you dirty looks from morning till night if he weren't going with the girl you want."

Tonio looked stung. "I really like her," he said with lowered eyes. "And Edwin is mean to girls. He won't be nice to her for very long."

"That may be, but if you really like this girl, you have to respect her ability to make her own decisions. Even one you think is bad."

"But what if he really is mean to her?"

Ramón pursed his lips. Here was a sticky wicket. "Unless he gets verbally abusive in public or actually hurts her physically, there aren't many options."

"That su— stinks."

"I know."

"Did you ever get a broken heart?" Tonio asked quietly.

Ramón looked out the window, remembering a day long ago, when a slim, pregnant teenager had stolen his heart. "Yes," he said. "It hurts every time. But eventually, you realize it won't kill you, even if it feels like it will."

Tonio sighed. "I hope so."

"Trust me, Antonio. Like any wound, it'll get better eventually."

The boy nodded. "Thanks, Dad. Can I go now?"

"Sure." He rubbed Tonio's arm. "Hang in there, kid."

After he left, Ramón swiveled to look out the window, thinking about wounded hearts and emotions running amok. He thought about kissing Tanya this afternoon. He couldn't remember the last time anything had made him feel so much. While their lips moved together, and he felt her hair on his hands, he'd felt dizzy, adrift. Alive like he hadn't been in a long time.

If the truth were told, he'd spent most of the day in a state of semiarousal. Everything set him off—her neat little hands, the movement of her small breasts beneath her shirt, the way she turned her head to look at the spines of books. Every move she made pleased him, aroused him, made him want to make love to her. Now.

But that state of arousal had less to do with a need to see or touch or kiss any particular body part—though he'd certainly enjoy nibbling a breast—than it did with Tanya herself. The woman she was, the woman she'd fought to save. The lean and wary survivor she'd become.

He'd told himself not thirty-six hours ago that he had to leave her alone. She needed time and space to sort out her life and options before she jumped into another relationship. She needed to live on her own and experience life without a man or the state making her decisions for her.

It killed him to think of it, though—think of her leaving the ranch after he'd waited so long to have her here. He liked the way she fit here. She was a good cook and a talented baker, but he was more impressed with her ability to mother all the lost boys in his care. They gathered around her like hummingbirds around four-o'clocks, taking nourishment from her calm voice and encouraging laughter.

For the sake of those boys, for the sake of Tonio, who would eventually learn Tanya was his mother, and for Tanya's sake, Ramón had to leave her alone. No more kisses. No more sexy teasing. None of it.

But a lonely, hungry voice in his head protested, She's the one! The One.

Tanya was right about the arm. It was painful the first night but felt much better the next day. By the time a week had passed, she not only didn't hurt anymore, but had grown so used to the stitches that she did everything she'd done without them. Soon she'd have to go to town to get them removed.

It was a peculiar week in many ways. The weather was brilliant—sunny and dry and warm. Indian summer. Her morning runs were exhilarating.

Tonio spent a lot of time in the kitchen, as did Zach. They talked, both of them, about everything and anything, as they peeled potatoes, or chopped carrots and tomatoes, or plucked freshly killed chickens of their feathers—a task Tanya particularly loathed. She'd grown used to eating animals she'd formerly seen running around the chicken coop, but didn't like being able to identify which particular chickens she was chopping into pieces.

There was one bad moment on a bright sunny afternoon. Although they sometimes played the radio, Desmary had complained of a headache and turned it off that afternoon. Outside were the sounds of other boys at their chores—feeding chickens and pigs, sweeping the barn. Tanya creamed brown sugar and eggs in a huge metal bowl while Tonio cracked walnuts from a huge bag someone had given them. It was tedious work, but he picked out nutmeats happily enough as long as he could nibble on some of them. It amazed her how much these boys ate—all of them nibbled, grazed, gulped, *ate*, all the time.

Tanya paused in her stirring to reach for vanilla and a measuring spoon, humming tunelessly to herself as was her habit. It had driven Victor around the bend, that humming, and yet she couldn't seem to drop it. It was a part of her, like having blue eyes or mousy brown hair.

One and a half teaspoons per batch, which meant four and a half teaspoons for this tripled recipe. She measured two and was pouring a third when Tonio demanded in a harsh voice, "What is that song?"

Tanya had to think. Which song was she humming today? An old folk song she'd learned at her one foray into camp when she was in sixth grade. "I don't know what it's called," she said with a grin. "We always called it 'There are suitors at my door.'" She sang the first line.

And remembered.

This song, along with "The Battle Hymn of the Republic," "The Ants Come Marching Home" and "The Cruel War," was part of her humming repertoire. It was the song Tonio had said he remembered his mother singing, the one about rivers running up hill and fish flying and a woman getting married the day before she died.

Tonio stared fiercely at her, his eyes ablaze with anger and hurt and a thousand questions. Standing there with the scent of vanilla in her nose, the notes of a song dying between them, Tanya willed him to remember, so the lie could be over. So she could stop tiptoeing around him. Softly she sang the last verse, the one he remembered.

"Stop it," he said fiercely. "Don't sing that song anymore."

"Why?" she asked quietly.

"I just hate it, that's all." He stood up violently, nearly knocking over the chair, and bolted out of the room.

With a shaky sigh, Tanya measured another teaspoon of vanilla and couldn't remember if she had added three or four. Better too little in this instance, she decided, and stirred it in.

She wondered how long it would be before he would guess. If he guessed—she supposed there was no reason for him to do so. Her hair was not long and blond anymore. Her body was lean and hard, rather than round and soft. Her name was Tanya, not the diminutive Annie he more than likely would remember.

And yet, the song was powerful. It was one she'd sung to him before bed every night. Every night. She'd even considered putting a tape of it inside the diaper bag she took to the day care woman's house that last night, but hadn't had time.

The incident disturbed her all afternoon. That evening, wearing a jacket over her sweatshirt, she sat on the back porch gutting pumpkins to be used as jack-o'-lanterns. The seeds she put in a huge bowl for roasting later.

The night was fresh and cool, smelling of distant leaf burnings and rustling grass. Indian summer in New Mexico was truly glorious. She loved being able to sit outside after dark in October.

The screen door creaked and Tanya glanced over her shoulder to see Ramón coming to join her. He carried two mugs of coffee, and put one down beside her on an overturned orange crate. "Thought you might like this," he said.

"Thanks."

He, too, had been a little odd this week. After the kisses last Saturday, she'd known a pleasurable sense of arousal and anticipation. But he steered clear of her, and at meals or other functions when he could not avoid her, he treated her like a sister, with friendly respect.

Now, dropping on to the old wooden chair near her own, he wrinkled his nose. "Aay, that stinks. I never liked the way pumpkin smelled."

"Me, either." Tanya shook her rubber-gloved fingers to loosen a long orange string. "Has to be done. Bet you like pumpkin pie."

"Not really."

"Not even with whipped cream?"

"Nope. Custard pies are disgusting. I used to have an aunt who made about thirty of them for every family gathering, and everyone else quit bringing pies because she baked so many, but they were all pumpkin or custard types."

Tanya smiled. "I don't remember anybody making pies when I was a child. There were no family gatherings, really. We moved so often we usually didn't even have any friends to invite over on holidays."

"Now that you say that, I realize I don't know much about your childhood. All I know about your parents is that they wouldn't help you when you...er.."

"Killed my ex-husband?" Tanya supplied dryly.

Ruefully, Ramón laughed. "Yes."

"They disowned me when I married him. I actually married him so early—" she had been one day past seventeen "—because they were moving and I was tired of going all the time. I never really had another conversation with them."

"I would say it's hard to imagine, but I've seen all kinds of parents in my line of work."

"Mine weren't all that terrible," she said. She so rarely thought of her parents it was as if they'd borne her in another lifetime. "I felt like I didn't belong with them."

"Was your father abusive?"

"No," Tanya said. It was not an uncommon question, coming as it did from a professional in the field. Often the children of abusive marriages grew up to repeat the pattern. "My dad was a philanderer. Slept with any woman he could get into bed. My mother responded by moving every time he formed an attachment. I went to sixteen schools by the time we made it to Albuquerque."

"And yet, with all of that, you turned out okay." He grinned, nudging her foot with his toe. "More or less."

Tanya smiled, halfheartedly, thinking of Tonio. She told Ramón what happened, then asked him, "What do you think he remembers? I mean about the way Victor acted."

Ramón took a breath. "He remembers some of it," he said quietly. "He used to wake up from his dreams screaming."

For a moment, Tanya considered asking what Antonio said after those nightmares, but she didn't think she could bear to know just now. "My poor baby."

"He's okay. He's a good kid."

"Yes, he is." And maybe, Tanya thought, he would forgive her the small duplicity she had practiced here. "Do you think we made a mistake by not telling him the truth about me?"

He stood up suddenly. "Come on, let's take a walk."

"Why?" She held up her gloved, pumpkin-stringed hands. "In case you haven't noticed, I'm kind of in the middle of something."

"I see." He reached over, grabbed the plastic table cloth from the table, and flung it over the pumpkins. "But it's important."

For a moment, Tanya measured him. Then she stood and stripped off the gloves. "All right," she said, and followed him down the steps into the moon-swept night.

Chapter Nine

Dear Antonio,
It came to me this morning that the man I killed was your father. I wonder if you hate me for that.

I also wonder if you're like him, and how. I wonder if you're starting to look like him as you get long-legged and lose your baby fat. I wonder how I'll feel if I see you and you're his spitting image.

Sometimes I go over that last time he found us, and I wonder what I could have done differently. I go over it and over it and over it. But we moved fourteen times in twenty months. We moved out of town. We moved into a house under an assumed name. I waited tables and dyed my hair. I signed restraining orders ... I did everything I could think of. And still he found us.

The time before the last one, he found us in Santa Fe, and he was furious. I hid you in our bedroom when I saw him coming up the walk, and closed the door. You screamed the whole time. I'll never forget it. After that, I kept wondering how long you would have been stuck in that room screaming if he'd actually killed me.

That's when I bought the gun. That fear made me decide it was time to take care of it myself, since no one else would. So I bought the gun and hid it and waited for him to find us again. When he did, I killed him. It wasn't the right answer, but it was the only answer I had left. I hope, if you hate me for what I've done, you'll remember that.

They tell me that if that had happened now, I wouldn't go to jail. I guess that's some comfort—that some other woman and some other boy won't have to pay the price we've paid here. I love you, son. I just want you to know that.

Love, Mom

The night was brisk, tasting of leaves and dry grass, and the peculiar notes of the desert itself, a pungent odor of juniper and sun-heated earth. Tanya tugged her jacket close around herself. "Okay, so you *do* think we made a mistake in not telling Tonio the truth?"

"No, that's just it—I know we didn't make a mistake. He might be upset when he learns the truth, but what I see is the two of you developing a real relationship, without all the entrapments of past history, at least on Tonio's part."

Tanya nodded slowly. A high moon lit the prairie with pale fingers, and lent a halo to Ramón's dark hair. His profile was hawkish against the night, that conquistadore's nose and high brow. A little shiver touched her, starting in her spine and radiating outward. She wanted him to kiss her again.

Actually, judging by her rather heated dreams, she wanted quite a bit more than kissing. They were almost embarrassing.

"I've been worried about it. About the fact that we're not telling the truth."

"Sometimes telling the whole truth only hurts people, Tanya. You know that."

She nodded.

He nudged her with his elbow. "You worry about everything. Maybe you should try to let some of it go. Those bags of guilt you're dragging behind you have to be pretty heavy some days."

Ruefully, Tanya smiled up at him, and made a motion as if she were taking a duffel bag off her shoulder to give him. "You want one?"

"No, thanks. I have plenty of my own."

"You? What do you have to be guilty and worried about?"

"Not guilty—though I do have a bag of that. Mostly I worry. About Tonio. About you." He gestured widely. "About all the boys."

Tanya pursed her lips, stepping carefully around a prickly pear spread around the foot of a yucca. Ramón made them all sound like part of some noble quest, as if he went around rescuing boys here and there, fishing them from the river of sin and sorrow. She frowned. "Am I one of your projects?" she asked. "Is Tonio?"

"No person is a project." His voice held a note of annoyance. "There are only people and I do the best I can with them. You were one of the people I wanted to see come through the system—somehow—okay. Most of these boys will die early deaths if I don't intervene, and some of them will no matter what I do." He looked at her. "But I have to try."

They stopped on a bluff overlooking the first finger of the Rio Grande—not nearly the formidable river it would become, but nonetheless a river with a certain authority. It clucked into the hollow made by a cottonwood's roots, and rushed over rocks. Tanya let go of a sigh she was unaware she was holding. "What about Tonio?" she asked, looking at the water. "Was he a project?"

He didn't answer immediately. His voice was thick when he spoke. "Tonio was born to you and Victor, but he's my son, Tanya. I've raised him for eleven years."

"I didn't mean—"

His mouth went hard. "Don't say it, Tanya. Just leave it out there. I am Tonio's father. He is my only child."

"I'm sorry. You didn't deserve that."

He looked at her but said nothing. They stood face-to-face on the open prairie, moonlight spilling down upon them like some narcotic perfume from a broken bottle. The light washed over Ramón's high cheekbones and touched his lips and the long brown strength of his throat. She ached to touch him.

He stared back at her, and Tanya felt his gaze lick her face and hair, her shoulders and breasts. Remembering his words in the bookstore, she said, "I really need to kiss you."

"We shouldn't, Tanya." But he moved a step closer, raising a hand to brush her hair off her shoulder. "I should leave you alone and let you find your own life, but I keep circling back to you, over and over again, like some lost sheep."

Tanya, made bold by his body language, if not his words, moved closer and put her hands on his waist under his coat. His sides were lean and warm below the cotton shirt, and she felt a shifting in the muscles when he took another step toward her. His arms circled her shoulders loosely and she let hers slide around to his back. Their bodies met lightly.

Their mouths joined. It was that simple and that clean. He bent and fit his mouth to hers. It wasn't so sweet this time. Tanya's body flushed as his mouth opened, as his sensual nature—so obvious in the way he touched everything and everyone, in his deep appreciation for beauty—overtook his cautious side. He made a low, warm noise and moved closer, and she felt his hard, flat belly against her own, felt his chest against her breasts. His lips moved in an expert dance of slow savoring, as if her mouth were more delicious than anything he'd ever tasted. Pleasure made her soft all over, in her knees, her hips, her hands that stretched open on his back.

His tongue ribboned the inner edges of her lips, and that part of her, too, was soft in response to him. She inclined her head slightly and let herself relax, giving him access to her mouth. A sharp bolt of almost overwhelming desire ripped through her when his tongue met hers, when they tangled so slowly, so deliciously. His hands moved on her back, and he pressed his hips to hers, and there was another jump in her nether regions.

Heaven, she thought vaguely. Heaven to kiss and kiss and kiss under a wide open sky filled with moonlight and the smell of crushed sage, and the tiny scratchings of hidden jackrabbits the only sound. Heaven to let her body mold closer and closer to his as the kiss deepened, intensified. Heaven to feel Ramón's strong hands reaching down to cup her bottom and urge her closer, to feel the ancient rocking movements between them.

She put her hands under his shirt and heard a hushed sound—delight and excitement—escape her throat. His skin was elegant satin, hot and smooth and delectably sensitive. He caught her lip and sucked on it, as if urging her to do more.

It had been such a long, long time. A powerful urgency built in Tanya's body, an ache too long left, and hunger so wild it seemed almost wanton. She moved her hands up his back, skimming his spine and the supple expanse of his muscles. Then, dangerously, she let her hands fall to the high, round rear end she had so often admired. He groaned and she pulled him closer, thinking nothing except that she would die if she had to stop.

A sudden noise in the darkness shattered the moment. An owl screeched and a small animal made a pained noise, and as if they'd been doused with water, Ramón and Tanya startled, clutching to each other in the primal, ancient fear of humans at the mercy of nature after dark.

They looked at each other, and Ramón lifted a hand to smooth Tanya's hair from her face. "It's La Llorona, the weeping woman, come to warn you."

"Warn me against what?"

He moved his body away from hers and took her hand. They walked alongside the river. "Do you know her story?"

"No."

"La Llorona guards the rivers—she was a very beautiful peasant girl who fell under the spell of a rich man. When he went to marry another, La Llorona threw their children in the river and drowned them, so he could have nothing, as she had nothing. Now she haunts the rivers, looking for her lost children, weeping and weeping."

Tanya felt a stinging recognition in the story. "How sad."

Ramón shrugged and lifted his face to the night, as if scenting the ghost. "It's a story to keep children away from the river," he said. "It isn't true."

A shiver ran down her spine. "You're wrong," she said quietly. "It is true. It's been true through all of time, and will be true a thousand years from now, and La Llorona is crying for all those women who were betrayed." Her voice roughened. "For me."

Ramón, who had stopped to listen, bent and put his mouth on hers again. It was a sharply heated kiss, filled with tongues and teeth and urgent need. Tanya met it eagerly, taking refuge in his sensual ways, in his demanding kiss. When he lifted his head, with a trail of one, two, three little kisses, he said, "I can't stop thinking about that, about kissing you." He brushed his lips over hers once more. "You know I think about it all the time, whenever I look at you?"

Watching his lips move, Tanya nodded, and drifted forward, her body alive and thrumming. She swayed toward him. "Don't be too hard on yourself," she said in a breathy voice, "I'm irresistible." She lifted her gaze and smiled.

"Two jokes in a single week? What's the world coming to?"

"I guess you're rubbing off on me."

He pressed against her, and Tanya pressed back. "Let's rub some more then," he said. And kissed her again. When the heat began to rise once more between them, Ramón put her firmly away. "I'm not Superman, cricket. Let's go back before I rip off your clothes right here."

Tanya backed away, and wiped her palms on her jeans. She lost herself when he kissed her. She just disappeared in pleasure.

In a companionable manner, Ramón tossed an arm around her shoulder and they walked back in the direction of the farmhouse. Tanya thought she could manage his proximity fairly well until she realized how her breast brushed his side. How their thighs touched, then didn't, then did. How his hips bumped hers. Yearning pulsed in her—the yearning to give herself to this sensual, sexy, gentle man.

With a cold sense of shock, she realized she was falling in love with him. How could that have happened? How could she have allowed her guard to slip so quickly?

As they reached the barn, Merlin came padding out and licked her hand. She bent and stroked his head. Ramón paused with her. The square was quiet. In the barn a horse nickered, and from the kitchen came the light clinking of spoons and pans and glassware. From the dorms came music, unidentifiable except for the pounding beat of rap, which seemed to be the music of choice for most of these boys. "I wonder why they like rap so much," she said aloud, trying to avoid her thoughts.

"It's angry," he said. "It expresses their feelings of betrayal and fury and violence."

"How can you approve?" Tanya asked. "It's misogynistic and violent."

"Some of it is," he said, lifting a shoulder. "So is a lot of rock and roll. Rap is like any other music—it expresses something that needs expression, whether we agree with the sentiment or not. And some of it is very powerful, very touching."

"Really?"

He nodded. "Ask Tonio to play some good songs for you. Tell him you want to learn about it. He'll show you."

"I will."

A small pause fell between them, empty, waiting for the words Tanya knew she needed to say. She took a breath, steeling herself, and said, "Ramón, I think you need to know I don't think I can give myself up to whatever this is between us. It scares me."

"Don't worry so much, Tanya."

She shook her head. "It isn't worry, Ramón. It's too intense. I just spent eleven years in prison because of an intense relationship."

"Not intense, Tanya—violent. There's a difference."

"Not to me."

His face was unreadable in the dimness, but she sensed his sudden stiffness. "I'm not Victor."

"I know that." And she did know. But they were alike in ways. There were similarities in the way they looked, and talked. The timbre of their voices was nearly the same. But most of all, the passion was the same.

No, that wasn't true. She had been so young when she and Victor got together that she'd never really even enjoyed sex all that much. Some of it was nice—the kissing and touching and all of that—but she had never liked it the way Victor did. She suspected, though of course she had no one to compare him to, that he had not been the most adept lover.

But then, he'd been very young too. And what he'd lacked in skill, he'd made up for in passion. "He wanted me so much I felt whole for the first time in my life," she said quietly. "He wanted to attach me to his body so that I'd be part of him. It's impossible to tell you how that made me feel."

"That's obsessive."

"I know," she repeated, and looked steadily at him. "I've fought so hard to be whole by myself, and when you kissed me like that . . . back there . . . I felt engulfed."

"Oh!" He sounded relieved. "Is that what's bothering you?" He lifted a hand to brush away a lock of hair from her face. "Do you think I was apart and coherent? Do you think anyone is at moments like that?" He shook his head. "They aren't."

Even his hand on her cheek made that pulsing heat burst through her body again, starting that ache low in her groin. Irritated, she turned her head. "I don't want that in my life. It's too crazy."

For a moment, his hand hung in midair. Slowly, he put it down, looking at her with measuring eyes. He nodded once. "I understand," he said. "I won't bother you anymore."

"Ramón! I didn't mean it like that."

He touched her arm, let it go. "I know you didn't." A sigh left him. "We'll just be friends, as we always have been." He cleared his throat, as if to change direction. "Will you help me put the dance together? We need to get it done—it's two weeks from this Friday."

"Of course," she said.

"Good." He lifted a hand. "See you tomorrow, then."

Tanya nodded, and clasped her arms around her chest. She should have been feeling relieved. She had seen the problem, confronted it as honestly as she could, and dealt with it. Why, then, did she feel such a sense of loss?

All the way into the house Ramón cursed himself. Or rather cursed everything—Victor, fate, timing. In his study, he closed the door and leaned against it.

Damn.

He had not intended to indulge himself like that, but out there in the moonlight, undone by the sweet yearning in her face, he had been unable to resist her. And even then, he'd only intended to play, to tease her a little and stoke the growing hunger he saw in her eyes. He'd meant to just take one more baby step forward into her skittish world. A light kiss, a few teasing words, a little light erotic play—kissing her palm, maybe, or her neck.

But the narcotic night had seduced him. Seduced Tanya. The moonlight had washed into them, and awakened their senses. Kissing her, he felt expanded—his hearing was so acute he heard the dance of field mice in their underground dens below the prickly pears, and scented the crush of juniper berries broken underfoot like spilled gin. He had closed his eyes, unwilling to add sight to the sensory overload, and concentrated on taste—her silky tongue, swirling with his, her eager lips, her faint sighs.

And feeling—her breasts bumping into his chest, immensely giving, her slim long back and round buttocks, firm with the muscles of her daily running.

He'd simply fallen over the edge at that moment, fallen adrift in the nectar of Tanya, in the pleasure of touching her, feeling her.

She was terrified, and with good reason. He had to keep himself in complete control. Not a single breach, or she'd run off like the wounded doe she was.

But he knew tonight that he could not let it lie any more. He wanted her deeply. She wanted him, too. It was right that he should be the one to teach her men were not all violent, that passion did not always wound. Perhaps he could help free her fully, to live instead of just survive. Slowly, carefully, he would show her. And if he had to let her go when she was free of the past, he would accept that, too.

The phone rang, and with a growl of frustration, he picked it up. It was the line from the dorms. "Ramón here."

"Dave here. We need you, stat." In the background were shouts and chaos. "Couple of boys are at it again."

"I'll be right there," Ramón said, and headed for the dorms, glad to have something to distract him.

Chapter Ten

Dear Antonio,

Sometimes now—from the great old age of twenty-seven—I think about how young we were, Victor and I, when we met. When we got married, when we each made decisions that would affect us forever. I was seventeen when we got married. Eighteen when you were born. At nineteen, I was already divorced. I met him when I was fourteen, and—well, never mind. No need for you to know every little detail.

Now I watch the news and see it's only getting worse. I see some of the young girls who come in here to visit their mothers or aunts or sisters—

and they're so old by the time they're fourteen. Already so grown up. And so often now, the boys just kill each other. Before they're even old enough to know how long forever is.

I wish we could make it better somehow for all of you. I hope Ramón will teach you to treasure your childhood, then your adolescence. Once it's gone, you can't be a kid ever again. Remember that. Be a child before you become a lover. Be a man before you take a wife.

Love, Mom

Tanya awakened from restless dreams long before the sun rose. A cat—this one named Snoopy—slept on her feet. It was a young orange-and-black calico, and stretched lazily when Tanya shifted to lie on her back while the dreams faded.

It was not uncommon for her to dream of the night of the shooting. She never remembered the actual moments—not the shooting itself or the police arriving. Her memory stopped with Victor at the bathroom door and picked up again when she was locked in a holding cell downtown with a prostitute wearing red fishnet stockings.

It wasn't uncommon for her to have nightmares of all kinds, actually. In her dreams, she worked out her sorrows and angst. In daily life, she thought she was fairly normal. It was only in her dreams that she reacted to everything that had happened.

As she lay there in the darkness, a cat purring on her chest as she stroked its soft, pointed ears, the dream she'd had filtered through her mind. It wasn't the last confrontation with Victor, or one of the other times he'd lost control or the more recent panicky dream of being back in prison.

No, this time, she'd dreamed of dancing with Ramón. He was younger, slim to the point of skinny, his glasses hiding his beautiful eyes. But his hands had been warm on her back, his laugh infectious and teasing, and his mouth—oh, she had seen his mouth that day. In her dream, she felt his arousal against her thigh, and she smiled up at him in a knowing, womanish way, to let him know she had noticed. In her dream, he had danced them toward a secluded cove and kissed her. Tanya laughed and put her arms around his neck, pulling him closer, kissing him deeply, reveling in the feeling of his hands on her breasts and smoothing over her rounded tummy.

Then she heard a shot, and Ramón slumped against her, his hot blood burning her hands that held the gun. In her dream, Tanya screamed, "No!"

And woke up to a cat on her feet in a room of Ramón's making. For the first time, she knew she'd dreamed a piece of that blacked-out day, as well as a metaphorical wish that things could have been different. If only she'd met Ramón sooner. Or been a little wiser about things. If only he had been a grown man instead of seeking boy.

If only.

With a sigh, she tossed back the covers and put on her robe. "If only" would make her crazy. No one had any clear idea of the world at seventeen. Victor had probably understood more, in his primitive way, than either Ramón or Tanya. Victor had sensed the powerful attraction between his cousin and his wife, an attraction neither Ramón nor Tanya had admitted.

She padded down the stairs in the silent house, going to the kitchen for a cup of tea. There was a light on already, and Tanya hung back, unwilling to meet Ramón in her present state. She needed to think about him and her feelings for him before the whole thing rocketed out of control. The kisses and touches between them had been, to this point, very gentle, but Tanya wasn't fooled. There was an untamed river of passion within Ramón Quezada, and it was dangerous to her carefully dammed emotions.

Silently, she peeked around the door and saw Tonio bent over a spiral notebook. A glass of juice and scattered evidence of varied snacks littered the table—popcorn, carrot sticks, an empty candy wrapper. He'd been there awhile. She wondered if she ought to leave him alone.

Pushing the door open, she said quietly, "Hi. Am I interrupting?"

Startled, he looked up at Tanya, then looked at the clock, which read 3:15. "What are you doing up?

"I could ask you the same question. Bad dreams?"

He quirked his mouth—and the gesture was utterly Victor. Somehow, it was a relief. This awkwardly teenage boy really was the Antonio she'd left behind, the one with the long eyelashes and a fondness for peanut butter crackers. "Nah," he said. "I just couldn't sleep."

Tanya took a mug from the cupboard. "I'm making some tea. Do you want some?"

"No, thanks." He pointed to his glass of juice.

"That should promote easy sleep, all right," she said, and smiled to show she wasn't criticizing. She filled her mug with water and put it in the microwave, then leaned against the counter, hands in her robe pockets. "Are you a writer?"

He shook his head, his thumb flipping the edge of his spiral notebook. The whole page was filled with his small, neat printing. "It's, like, a letter."

The microwave dinged. Tanya took out her mug and fixed the tea. "I'll leave you alone, then," she said.

"You don't have to," he said. "I mean, you don't have to stay and keep me company, either, but I don't mind if you're in here."

Tanya took the hint and sat down, trying to find someplace for her eyes besides the white, heavily filled page. His hair, freshly washed and as yet unslicked, hung black around his face—a face that was angled and brown and beautiful, all the more startling because of his blue eyes. Her eyes, she thought proudly.

Eyes presently filled with misery. "Still feeling bad over the girl—was her name Teresa?"

"Yeah." Restlessly, he flipped his pen onto the page, off the page. "I really like her. And I know Edwin's gonna hurt her—maybe not outside, but he'll hurt her. He's a jerk."

Tanya carefully schooled her mouth to keep her opinions to herself. It wouldn't do to say, "You're right—he is a jerk." Instead she lifted a shoulder. "Maybe. But maybe he really likes her, too." She held up a hand at his protest. "I know you don't want to hear that, but it just might be true."

Tonio stubbornly shook his head. "He's already said he slept with her. I heard him saying it in the orchard that day. He's lying. She wouldn't do that."

Again, to remain neutral, Tanya nodded, sipping her tea. "It sounds like a tough situation."

"You know those really jealous guys who beat up everybody when they think their girlfriend is talking to someone else or something?"

"Sure," Tanya said, tongue in cheek.

"He's like that. He almost killed his own brother over some girl back in Albuquerque, and I saw him hit a girl last spring for calling him a name."

None of the anecdotes surprised her, but Tanya still didn't know what the best advice for Tonio would be. "Have you tried to talk to her? Maybe she just doesn't realize how dangerous he might be."

"You believe me."

Tanya nodded.

He put his hand on his hip, pushed the notebook an inch up on the table. "I'm writing her a letter."

"Good." She bit her lip. To say any more would be foolish.

"I tried not to say anything about how I feel about her or anything. I just want her to be safe from Edwin—he only wanted her to get to me, anyway." Again he flipped his pen restlessly on the page. "I'm only going to tell her one time I'm here for her if she needs me."

"That seems a very wise choice."

Tonio looked at her. "Sometimes, it's so easy to talk to you, it's like I know you already. Like I knew you when you came here."

Tanya froze. Did he guess who she was? Was she ready for that? He didn't seem angry. "Sometimes people just mesh. I've met people I hated on sight, too."

Color moved up his cheeks and he lowered his eyes. "I think you kinda remind me of my mom. She gave me away when I was three, to Ramón."

Words burned in her throat—words she desperately wanted to say. *I am your mother and I didn't give you away, you were taken.* To hold them back, she didn't speak, only sipped some tea and swallowed the words, bitter and whole, nodding. One thing she'd learned early in life was that people only needed a little nodding to keep talking.

Tonio included. "She was real young. It was probably too much for her—though my dad, that is, Ra-

món, says she wanted to keep me out of all the mess."
He rubbed the paper under his hand. "I have one
letter she wrote to me before she had to go to prison."

In a swift bright flash, Tanya was sitting in her
kitchen in the little house in Albuquerque, amid the
ruins of her carefully collected, hand-painted and
mismatched china, writing a letter. She could see her
hand on the paper, writing "Dear Antonio..."

"That must be comforting," Tanya said over the
ache in her chest. It amazed her how calm her voice
sounded. "It's nice that you kept it."

"It's all I have."

She smiled, honestly this time. "It's more than
Zach has, isn't it?"

Tonio's expression lightened. "Yeah," he said.
"Yeah, it is."

"Well," she said, picking up her cup. "I'll leave
you to your letter."

He nodded. "Thanks for listening, Ms. Bishop."

"My pleasure." Tanya walked cooly to the door,
but just beyond, she bolted. No way this could go on
much longer. No way. Every time he gave her a
chance to confess and she didn't, the lie got bigger.
Every time she pretended not to be his mother, he
would remember when the truth was revealed.

With a feeling very much like panic, Tanya went to
Ramón's room. She tapped at the door and waited,
her arms crossed on her chest. Nothing. She tapped
again, and called him softly, although he was alone
on the second floor. "Ramón!"

A groggy voice answered her. "Come in."

Within, the darkness was absolute. Tanya closed the door behind her and stumbled forward, propelled by her panic. "Ramón?" she whispered, and tripped over a pair of jeans.

"Straight ahead," he mumbled, sleepily.

Tanya moved forward gingerly, hands outstretched. The room smelled of his skin, of him, rich and faintly spicy. The front of her thighs struck the bed and she bent over involuntarily, her hands going out to stop herself.

One palm landed on his stomach—bare and hot. The other landed on the pillow near his head. His thick coarse hair brushed her inner wrist. Hastily she straightened, rubbing her hand restlessly against her leg.

Now that she stood here, the intense reality of the moment came to her. She smelled his skin and heat, and the knowledge that his torso—at the very least—was bare, made her palms burn and her breasts ache. "This was a mistake," she whispered. "I'll leave you alone. I'm sorry. I don't know what—"

A big hand snagged her wrist, and Tanya tumbled forward, landing on the bed next to him. "You don't have to rush off." His voice was rough with sleep. "I've only been in bed a half hour, so another few minutes isn't going to make any difference."

"No, I—this was—I'm sorry." She tried to move away, embarrassment flooding her. What had she been thinking? She hadn't been thinking. Only feeling. "I'll leave you alone."

"Come here and tell me what's wrong."

Waves of mortification washed through her. "No, really, Ramón—"

He tugged her again. "Lie down here with me, cricket. Let me hold you." He pressed his mouth to her hand. "Just for a minute."

Tanya resisted one more moment, but his scent permeated the room, filling her with a restless sense of need. Knowing even as she relented that it was a mistake, she gingerly eased her body down beside him.

"That's it," he said roughly, and tucked an arm around her. The heat of his length along her body gave her a wild jolt. "Tell me what's bothering you, *grillacita*."

She remembered what had driven her here. "I have to tell Tonio the truth."

"Mmm." Lazily, his hand moved on her body as he nestled closer to her, his chest against her arm, his face tucked against her neck. The broad hand made a wide circle over her stomach, up an arm, lightly clasped a breast, then moved quickly away before she could protest. Against her buttocks pressed his arousal, pointed and hot below the covers. She was almost sure he slept with no clothes—clothes would make that feel different. Her breath caught as his mouth landed against her shoulder.

"Pretty soon, we'll tell him," he said with a rasp, and his hand slipped inside her robe, over her thin nightgown, and stroked her breast again. Her nipples leapt to full attention. His skillful fingers circled back, touched the aroused points lazily, slowly. "Soon," he said into her hair. His mouth touched her neck, hot and moist. Tanya shuddered, feeling arousal rush through her.

He planted a kiss on the vulnerable flesh below her ear, and his tongue teased the edge of her ear. She made a low noise and closed her eyes, trying to be still so she wouldn't give herself away. He felt so good, he smelled so good....

The questing fingers freed two buttons on her gown and slid inside, and all at once, his naked fingers were touching her breast, skin to skin, and she gasped. He swirled and skimmed and cupped, teasing her nipple as his mouth moved on her neck, her ear, her jaw. Lower, his hips moved against her bottom, and she found herself responding with movements of her own. A warm, pleased sound came from his throat.

He spread kisses up the side of her neck. "Turn over, sweetness, let me kiss you properly."

Tanya needed no second urging. She turned in his embrace and found him propped on one elbow, ready to bend and kiss her. Lightly, so lightly. With his free hand he unbelted her robe and flipped it open. She shivered.

His big hand stroked her breasts, then opened the rest of the buttons and spread open the gown. She felt the air against her breasts an instant before he moved his hand to clasp and caress her flesh. As his tongue opened her lips and plied her mouth, he moved his deft fingers to the points of her breasts and played there, teasing and stroking. He opened his mouth and invited her in, and Tanya entered the sacred cavern, and found herself arching against his plucking fingers, his thrusting tongue.

He made a low, dark noise. "We aren't going to make love tonight," he whispered, "because I'm not prepared, and neither are you, but there's no reason we can't do some heavy petting, is there?" In illustration, he roved over her breasts deliciously, heating her flesh with his touch. "Do you know a reason?"

She put her hands on his naked back, nearly breathless with the pleasure of it. "No reason I can think of."

"Good," he breathed. With exquisite slowness, he bent his head and put his mouth on her breast. He touched the tip lightly with his tongue. She gasped. Deliciously, he tortured her with more light flutters that sent shooting arrows of sensation through her body. Urgently, she put her hands in his thick, gloriously wavy hair, and reveled in the sensation against her fingers, silky and cool and heavy all at once. And his mouth, so hot and wet, suckled her, lightly, then more fiercely, as if he were starving. His hand moved on her body, skimming her waist and thighs, and she felt the brush of hair as he tugged her gown up and skimmed her thighs with an open palm. "Tanya," he breathed, kissing her, "you're so sweet. So sweet."

And in her turn, Tanya tasted his neck, his throat, his slightly prickly chin. She slid her tongue over the long dark column of his throat into the hollow at the base, where she could feel the pulse of his life moving, beating. He was so hot—his skin was like the dark pelt of an animal who had been sleeping in the sun—and it warmed the cold, lost places inside of her.

Somehow, her robe and panties were shed, and Ramón's hands grew urgent on her body, his kiss hot and intense. She skimmed the blanket from his body and found he was indeed bare beneath it, and she put her hands on his hips, glorying in the muscled feel against her palms.

Ramón touched her, from shoulder to knee, with his hands, and his mouth, and then he covered her with his body, the lower half still draped in a sheet, and she wanted to weep with the feeling of that sleek, naked chest moving lightly over her bared breasts. He kissed her deeply, hungrily, and she thought she would die of pleasure and need.

And then, oh, then, he slipped his hand between her legs and stroked her, only a little, ever so expertly, exactly as she would have asked him to, if she had dared. The deep heat that had been growing low in her abdomen over days of kisses and dreams simply exploded.

It was not like anything else.

She had never experienced the true pinnacle of sex, and the experience was unbelievable, inexpressible, outrageous. She heard a low, dark moan rise into the room, and realized it was coming from her own throat, as wave after wave rocked her. After long moments of blinding pleasure, the waves slowed and faded, but Ramón made a small, joyful sound and bent his head to her breast, where he teased and lapped and nibbled, and the rocketing waves returned.

Never, never, never had she understood, she thought, overcome. As the waves subsided, leaving a wide rippling heat in her body, she knew an empty aching—and that was a sensation she recognized. She needed Ramón inside of her. She urged him closer, and he kissed her, but didn't take her invitation.

"No," he whispered finally. "I'll wait my turn. I have no condoms here. I have to buy them."

Tanya, shaking, knew there were ways to give him what he'd just given her, but she was too weak, too deeply sated. He settled next to her, his hand over her breast. "Sleep, my sweet."

And Tanya, exhausted by sexual satisfaction for the first time in her life, did just that.

Ramón awakened the next morning, his body tight and aching with desire. Against him, Tanya slept, just as he'd imagined so many times. Her hair, shiny and clean-smelling, tumbled over her cheek, and her pretty, soft mouth was almost unbearably lush in sleep. One white breast, unbelievably beautiful, was exposed.

Moving cautiously, he reached for the cover to pull it up over her, to cover her nudity. But she shifted in his arms, still soundly sleeping, and the movement put one pert, rosy nipple almost next to his mouth. He groaned and closed his eyes, willing his desire to some faraway place, but her skin was soft against him, and his breath caused her nipple to pearl, and he rationalized the heavens would not so irresistibly tempt him if he wasn't meant to act.

With a sigh, he bent his head and accepted the sweet fruit into his mouth, savoring the taste for the delicacy it was. He suckled until he felt her stir, moaning softly. Her hands fell first in his hair, and her fingers roved over his scalp. She whispered his name in a voice soft with wonder and delight, and her hands moved on his body.

She touched him. Intimately, hotly, embracing his aching shaft firmly, moving in the ancient rhythm, and he forgot himself, forgot that he was a calm grown man who could hold off until there was protection, who could resist anything.

He couldn't resist Tanya. Couldn't resist this.

She coaxed him to satisfaction, and didn't flinch when he grasped her arms and kissed her deeply. And when the violent rocking had finished, he gathered her close. Touched her delicate ears, her beautiful breasts, the hungry tips, and the sleek flat of her stomach, moving lower. She stopped him, and whispered breathily, "Let's wait, until we can make love properly." She opened her eyes. "I want all of you."

Ramón kissed her. "Tanya, I missed you." A thick pulse filled his groin, making him ready again. "I'll never be able to keep my hands off you today."

She smiled. "You'd better. There are a lot of boys down there looking up to you."

"I promise I'll illustrate the right way to touch a woman for them. Will that help?"

"No." She slapped his arm. "I can't believe I never before knew what was supposed to happen."

"I don't know what you mean."

"You know." Her voice dropped and a hot pink stain touched her cheekbones. "The whole enchilada."

He thrust his hips at her playfully. "No, you haven't had the whole enchilada, baby. Not yet."

"Ramón!" She ducked her head into his shoulder and mumbled a word into his neck.

"Orgasm!" he said, pulling back to look at her face. "You've never had an orgasm before?"

She shook her head.

Ramón smiled, broadly. "Oh, cricket, are we going to have some fun." He kissed her. "Tonight."

A flush touched her face again, but it wasn't embarrassment this time. Her eyes were awash with liquid heat. "Better find a way to hide that glow, or I'll have to reassign you. Those randy boys will catch fire."

"No," she whispered, lifting her arms around his neck. "Just keep the fire low, and we'll be fine."

"My pleasure." He kissed her, wondering how he'd fallen into such good fortune, so suddenly. "My pleasure."

Tanya moved through breakfast preparations feeling as if the world were covered with a sheer coating of pearlescent light. Everything glowed. She glowed, and she knew it, and she tried to hide it.

But she was so aware of her body this morning it was nearly impossible. As she blended ingredients for bread, she felt the press of clothes against her breasts, as if the cotton were too heavy, and her arms felt tingly, as if they were waiting, and the dark pulse low in her abdomen jolted her every time she thought of the night, of Ramón touching her... kissing her... stroking her body to such heights!

She'd almost forgotten the middle of the night conversation with Tonio until he came into the kitchen after breakfast. He showed her an envelope. "I'm gonna give it to her today," he said. "If I come home with a broken face, you'll know she showed it to Edwin."

She hadn't considered that end, and some protective motherly instinct made her say, "Maybe you should reconsider. You don't want to get hurt."

A scowl crossed his face. "That's what's wrong with this world—everybody talks about making it a better place, but nobody ever wants to stick their own neck out." He put the letter into his book bag. "Well, I'm not gonna look the other way."

"You're right," Tanya said, and put her hand on Tonio's arm. "You're doing the right thing." She smiled. "But somebody has to do the worrying for the ones who do the right thing."

"I'll be okay."

"I know you will."

He stood there one more minute, looking down at her with his deep blue eyes in their frame of sooty lashes, and he was so beautiful it made her heart hurt. An odd flicker passed over the vibrant irises, and Tanya wondered again if he guessed who she really was. "Well," he said, "see ya."

"Good luck."

Tonio nodded and left, and for the first time, Tanya saw that his walk, too, belonged to Victor—a long-legged lope.

"Why," Tanya said to Desmary, watching him walk toward the bus stop, "would any girl in her right mind choose Edwin Salazar over a boy like Tonio?"

Desmary looked past Tanya to the road. "Bad boys are more exciting."

Tanya nodded. Who had she chosen, after all? She turned to look at the old woman. "I find myself wanting to teach them, somehow, those girls. Teach them how to choose a man who is worthy of them." On a rising tide of regret and worry, she punched the dough in her bowl. "I want to wash their faces so their pretty skin shines through, and put them in clothes that don't make them look like twenty-year-olds." She paused to look at Desmary. "I want them to know they don't have to give themselves away."

"It will come, child," Desmary said. "You'll be a fine teacher for them, when it's time. Don't be in too much of a hurry. You have things of your own to work out."

"I know." Tanya smiled. "And I have you to teach me."

"Long life doesn't necessarily make a woman wise."

"That's true. But I think you were born wise."

"No, child." Desmary sighed, and her eyes wore a faraway look. "I earned every morsel of everything I ever knew. The hard way, just like everybody else."

Tanya smiled. "The way I'm learning it."

Desmary seemed to bring herself into focus. "He knows, I think."

"Knows what? Who?"

"Tonio knows—or is beginning to guess—that you are his mother."

A cold finger stabbed her chest. "Why do you say that? Did he say something to you?"

"No. I just sense it."

With a sigh, Tanya nodded. "I think so, too."

"Are you ready for it?"

"I don't know," she replied. "I honestly don't know."

Chapter Eleven

Dear Antonio,
I'm in a work camp now. It's not nearly as restrictive as either of the other places. We work outside sometimes, and for the first time, I can see the horizon.

Every now and then lately, I realize I might really get out of here someday. I might really see you again.

I wrote to Ramón a few weeks ago. It wasn't easy to find him, actually, but one of the Sisters who come out here to teach and minister helped me track him down. I guess you're living on a ranch now. I haven't heard from him yet, but I guess he hasn't had time, either. I feel anxious, wondering if he'll help me talk to the right people to get the restriction against seeing you lifted. The lawyer I talked to here said I have a good chance of getting it overturned. The climate for women who have committed crimes like mine is very different now.

It made it real to me, writing to Ramón. Made me try to imagine how you might look now, at fourteen. I imagined you on a horse, looking like your dad when I first met him. That probably isn't too far from the truth.

With high spirits and lots of love, Mom

About 2:00, Ramón came into the kitchen. "Desmary, can I steal your helper this afternoon? I want to get her input on some more plans for this dance."

"About time, I'd say," Desmary replied. "You only have ten days."

"There isn't that much to do! You have the food covered, right?"

"Only a little—you haven't given me any menus."

"I'll take care of the rest," Tanya said. "Make a list of what you've already planned, and I'll fancy up the rest."

"Good girl." Desmary swiveled on her stool—she had everything set up so she had to stand or walk as little as possible—and tugged out a scrap of paper and a pencil. She licked the pencil and started scribbling.

"What else needs taking care of?" Tanya asked Ramón. She met his eyes, and blushed feverishly at the look in them. Wickedly, he winked.

"The counselors have taken care of the invitations, the letters to parents, both at the school and here. Any girl who comes out here has to have parental permission."

"Will any of them give it?" Tanya asked.

"What do you think? We have a bus going to town to pick them up and one to take them back. The parents don't have to do a thing." He watched Desmary writing. "We have to read it, *abuelita*."

"I can read it," Tanya said, as Desmary smacked his arm.

"We have to come up with decorations and music and maybe some kind of game, so we can give prizes. I've got movie passes and roller skating passes. We ought to come up with something else, too."

"Okay." Tanya inclined her head. "Why not a dance contest or something like that?"

"That might work."

Desmary handed the list of food to Tanya, who scanned the paper quickly and folded it to put in her jeans pocket. "Sure you'll be all right without me?"

A bright twinkle brightened Desmary's eyes. "I'm fine. You two go on."

"Good."

Tanya fetched her jacket and purse from her room, and met Ramón on the front steps. "Ready."

"Me, too," he said in a husky voice.

Tanya smiled.

Edwin was in the yard, raking leaves beneath the path of cottonwoods that lined the road to town. He paused to salute ironically at the pair of them. "Don't forget to bag the leaves," Ramón called.

Edwin lifted an orange trash bag, printed with a jack-o'-lantern. "Gotcha."

As they climbed into his truck, Tanya asked Ramón, "Why isn't Edwin in school?"

"He has been suspended. And last night, there was an altercation in the dorms. Guess who was at the center of it, as usual?"

"Ah."

"He's right on the edge. Won't be long now till he either hangs himself with his behavior and ends up in the state detention center, or realizes he doesn't have a prayer unless he straightens up."

"I know where I'll put my money," Tanya said darkly.

"You really don't like him, do you?"

"No, I really don't. Gut instinct."

"Well, I'm obligated to see that he gets the same chance as everyone else."

"I know. I wasn't suggesting he should have less of a chance." She pursed her lips, wondering if she ought to mention the letter Tonio had written to Teresa. She had the feeling Tonio had spilled his emotions to her because he trusted her to say nothing, and since Edwin wouldn't be in school today, perhaps there would be no trouble over the letter anyway. She chose to keep quiet.

About a mile from the ranch, Ramón pulled the truck over under a copse of lonely trees.

"What are you doing?" Tanya asked.

"This." He moved out from behind the steering wheel and slid over the bench seat until Tanya was neatly trapped between him and the door. She smiled up at him. "You're making me a sandwich?"

"Only if I can eat you," he said with a wicked lift of one dark brow. His lips claimed hers, wet and hungry and sensual. "Mmm," he said, rubbing her arm. "I've been dying to do that all morning."

"Maybe I ought to cool you down, then," Tanya teased in return, and stuck her cold hands under his shirt.

He jumped. "I'll get you for that, woman."

"I'm real scared."

The dark eyes sobered, and he touched her face. "Never be afraid of me, cricket. Not ever."

Tanya gripped his shirt front, thinking of what she'd told Desmary this morning about young girls. This was the sort of man she wanted for all the women of the world—a kind man, a good one, who could love children and tend animals and make love like Casanova himself. What more could any woman ask than Ramón Quezada? "I'll never be afraid of you, Ramón." She kissed him, her eyes open so she didn't have to stop looking into the depths of those rich, promising eyes.

His hand, cold as her own, snaked under her sweater and bra and closed on her breast. Tanya squealed and tried to squirm away. "Paybacks," he said, and laughing, kissed her quickly, then let her go.

The afternoon was filled with the same kind of teasing, all of it edged with a giving sensuality Tanya had never experienced. With Victor, sex had been a dark and deadly serious thing.

Not so with Ramón. At the library, he stood behind her, very close, and, making sure no one could see him, bent to nibble her ear until her knees were weak. He caught her in a deserted section and pressed her back against the wall and kissed her senseless, then walked away whistling as if he'd done nothing. At the restaurant where they stopped for coffee, he leaned over and whispered naughty descriptions of what he wanted to do to her body when he got her alone again. Tanya blushed, but his words were poetically couched and never crude—the pictures they made in her mind made her hips soft.

Under the table, she teased back, letting her hand drift higher and higher on his leg as he talked. When she neared her destination—then stopped just short— his whispering ceased and Tanya looked up mischievously. "You were saying?"

He laughed.

They stopped by the clinic so Tanya could have her stitches removed, and the cut looked red and raw, but she could tell it would be fine. A thin scar might remain, but not much of one.

The last stop was the drugstore. Tanya waited in the truck while he went in. Teenagers, recently released from school, milled in the streets of the small town. Some of them hung on the corner talking, in the ancient tradition of those too young or too poor to drive. A gaggle of girls, their eyes lined with thick black liner, hair teased over their foreheads, walked together toward the drugstore. A young couple, a slim small girl and a long-limbed boy, strolled down the street, in no hurry to be anywhere. Tanya watched them, caught in their yearning discomfort. The boy leaned close, then away. The girl swayed his direction, then caught herself. From the back, it was impossible to tell how old they were. Tanya smiled when the boy managed to capture the girl's hand, and she looked up at him, and they kissed, awkwardly at first, then with more passion.

Tanya glanced away, unwilling to intrude. But a small detail of something snagged her peripheral vision and she glanced back. The backpack the boy carried had a large green political button pinned to it—and Tanya knew just what it said: Save the Rain Forest.

It was Tonio. Now she could tell, even at this distance, even though his clothes and hair were the same as a half a dozen other boys on the street. No doubt the girl was the infamous Teresa, who looked impossibly small to be the center of such a tempest.

Ramón climbed back in the truck and patted his pocket with a wicked lift of his eyebrows. When Tanya didn't respond, he said, "What is it?"

She lifted her chin and gestured in the traditional Southwestern method of avoiding the rude point of a finger. "Tonio."

Ramón caught sight of the pair and sighed. "Ah, hell." He watched them, pursed his lips, swore again. "He's supposed to be at debate club this afternoon."

"What are you going to do?"

He shook his head. "There's no law against him taking a girl to get a soda, but I hate to think he's been lying to me."

"I don't think he has. That's surely Teresa, and she's been going with Edwin."

"How do you know so much about this?"

"Tonio talked to me about it."

Ramón measured her. "And you didn't say anything?"

"Say what, Ramón? He wanted to talk to a woman about a girl, and I was handy, that's all."

With a pensive expression, Ramón watched Tonio and Teresa join hands once more and head for the ice-cream shop on the corner. They were smiling at each other as they went inside. "I don't like this situation. At all."

Tanya shook her head. "It's trouble, all right."

"Damn." Ramón started the truck and backed out.

* * *

Ramón felt choked as they drove back to the ranch. His earlier mood of sexy playfulness evaporated, killed by the specter of the possible danger Tonio had put himself in. Or maybe the danger Ramón had put him in—because if he hadn't had his heart set on running this ranch for troubled boys, Tonio wouldn't be in this position.

Not like this.

Ramón also felt guilty about the fact that he'd been buying condoms for himself when he was about to give Tonio the standard lecture about sex.

It was true he was an adult, and therefore capable of making decisions that were beyond the capacity of a fourteen-year-old. It was also true that Ramón had not given enough thought to the consequences of a sexual relationship with Tanya. It was his libido that was engaged, his libido turning him into a version of a randy teenager. He'd been completely unable to keep his hands off her today, had thought of nothing but getting her into his bed tonight and making love to her thoroughly and completely.

He'd given no thought to what would come afterward. And when he'd seen Tonio kissing his girlfriend, a vision of himself kissing Tanya in the library flashed before his eyes.

Do as I say, not as I do.

That had never been the way Ramón did things. He believed in the old-fashioned method of providing an example for boys to emulate, not setting down a list of arbitrary rules. He didn't drink, not because he had problems with it, but because so many boys did. He didn't smoke, even though he missed it, because he wanted to be a good role model. When he had carried on his affair with the teacher in town, he'd been very discreet, and careful to handle everything away from the ranch.

But with Tanya, he'd lost control. She had come to his room trustingly to tell him something, and he'd seduced her, knowing she was vulnerable, that she was ripe to be made love to, that she needed it.

Nice justification.

On the far end of the bench seat, Tanya sat with crossed arms, staring with no expression out the window. A sorrow pierced him. There was no possible way to keep such a thing secret at the ranch. The boys would start gossiping about her. They might even make remarks to her face.

And that would hurt her.

In sudden decision, he pulled over, this time on a lonely stretch of naked road. Across a vista of dry prairie grasses and swords of yucca, the mountains were a jagged blue line under a frosting of clouds. He turned off the engine and sat quietly, trying to think of the right way to word his thoughts.

"Tanya," he began.

She looked at him, her vulnerable deep blue eyes wide in her face, a face that showed the strength of her in ways he doubted she even guessed. The authority of experience lived in the cut of her mouth. The courage that had seen her survival burned in her eyes. Character had painted a face of honor and sensitivity.

He closed his eyes. Somehow these past few weeks, he had fallen in love with Tanya Bishop. Not the infatuation of a randy boy, but the sustained and powerful love of a man who had learned what was important in a mate. Tanya had everything he ever hoped to find.

And if things were different, if fate had not cheated them so cruelly, he might have been able to say to her now, "Marry me." A marriage would be a good thing for the boys at the ranch to see, an honorable, passionate union between a man and a woman. At the thought, he felt a deep and powerful yearning to make it so.

But it wasn't fair to use Tanya's long unfulfilled hunger to be complete for his own ends. He could make love to her until she was senseless—heaven knew how much he wanted that—but she wasn't the kind of woman to take sex lightly.

Nor was he that kind of man. When he'd imagined making love to her tonight, it had been with the wish that they become one, that they create a precious and mighty union of souls.

If he actually made love to her, if he allowed them to be joined, allowed the mingling of souls that would accompany such an act for them, he would never have the strength to let her go and find her own life.

"We're going to have to cancel our appointment for tonight," he said at last.

"I know." Her voice was resigned.

"It isn't for lack of—"

"Ramón, please don't go into all kinds of explanations. Let's just leave it at this. There are complicating factors we both understand."

He caught her and tugged her close to him, putting his face against her hair. She clung to him, and he felt her take a huge, shuddering breath. "I want you, Tanya," he said into her neck. "I wanted to teach you—"

Abruptly, she lifted her head and covered his mouth with her fingers. Cold fingers. "No more. I don't want to hear any more."

She extricated herself and scooted back to her place by the window.

Ramón, feeling the weight of a box of condoms in his pocket, started the truck and drove back to the ranch. It was the right decision, the moral decision, but that didn't mean he had to like it.

An almost palpable glow hung around Tonio that evening. Ramón kept his peace throughout supper, but afterward, he asked Tonio to stay when Tanya got up to help in the kitchen. In a minute, she came back with a steaming mug of coffee for him. She set it before him, and asked Tonio if he wanted anything. When he refused, she faded away.

Some women rebelled at performing such chores for men. Some women would also find Tanya's acceptance of work in the kitchen degrading. But she seemed to take joy in the small gestures that made people comfortable—she liked taking care of people, tending them, making their lives easier. A rare and precious thing.

"What's up, Dad?" Tonio asked, shaking Ramón from his reverie.

Ramón cleared his throat and hunched forward over his coffee, putting his hands around the heat of the mug. "Did you have practice this afternoon?"

Instant guilt shuttered Tonio's features. "Uh, no."

"You were pretty late home, if you didn't go to practice. What did you do?"

Tonio frowned. "Why do I get the feeling you already know?"

Ramón sipped his coffee.

"I went to Fiddler's for an ice-cream soda. That's not so bad."

"No. Except I thought you were at practice. What if something had happened, and I needed to find you right away?" He sighed and shook his head—he promised himself he'd be honest with this child whenever he could. "That's not even the real problem for me, Tonio, although I wish you'd remember to call when you change your mind about where you'll be."

"Sorry."

"I saw you in town," Ramón said. "With the girl. Is that Teresa?"

Faint color gave warmth to Tonio's dark skin. "Yeah."

"I don't want to stick my nose in where it doesn't belong, son, but—"

"Then don't."

"I have to. You're not thinking with your head, but with your emotions. Emotions can get you into trouble."

"They won't. I'm not!" He shoved back from the table in frustration and looked away. But he didn't quite dare to leave, and that was a good thing.

"How do you think Edwin is going to react when he hears about it? And why do you want to be with a girl who can't make up her mind?"

"She can make up her mind. She's coming to the dance with me."

"Yesterday, she was going to be Edwin's date."

"That was before I told her—"

"Told her what?"

"Nothing." Tonio shook his head. Arcs of light caught in the glossy blackness of his hair. "Just leave me alone, okay?" He jumped up.

"Sit down."

Tonio sat, mutinously staring at Ramón.

"It's not just the fighting I worry about," Ramón said quietly. "I worry about you getting in over your head with this girl."

"Over my head?" he sneered.

Ramón eyed him. "I'm talking about sex, Antonio. It's too important to take lightly."

Tonio bowed his head, and Ramón knew he was right to bring it up. The thought—maybe more than the thought—had crossed the boy's mind.

"I'm not naive enough to believe you'll hold out forever, but I wish you would take time to really think it through. Sex is deep, Antonio. It's supposed to bind you to another person, soul to soul, and anything else makes it cheap."

Tonio didn't speak. He kept his head bowed.

"Just promise me you'll think about it."

The boy nodded. "I will."

"I trust you to do the right thing, you know."

"Thanks." Tonio stood up. "Can I go now? I have some homework to do."

"Sure."

A sharp gust of wind struck the farmhouse as Tonio ambled out of the room. Ramón heard the windows rattle and wondered if it would snow. It would suit his mood.

Body to body. Soul to soul. Binding and deep and important. He sipped his coffee and sighed. He wished so much for that joining with Tanya that he could barely breathe. He wanted to meld with her, become one with her. He wished there was some way to do it fairly.

Damn. He didn't want Tanya to go anywhere or find any other life. He wanted her to take the place he had for her here, in his life, in his heart, next to him.

But he couldn't ask it. Not yet. Not until she'd had some time to find her own life first. It wouldn't be fair.

Fair. What a mockery life always seemed to make of that word.

Chapter Twelve

Dear Antonio,

I saw the parole board today. They are going to let me go. I can hardly believe it. And as if that weren't enough joy for one day, Ramón has written to say it was never his wish that you and I be separated. He offered me a job at the ranch, cooking, when I'm done with the program at the halfway house. It's hard to believe I will actually see you again one day soon.

Love, Mom

On the night of the dance, Tanya dressed carefully.

Her thoughts were on Ramón, and his decision to not have sex with her. She pretended to accept it.

But her body had not accepted his decision. The night they'd seen Tonio in town with his girlfriend, when Ramón had so hastily retreated, Tanya had lain awake for hours, her body on fire. She wanted to make love to him, as they'd planned. She wanted to hear his low groans, and touch his hair and feel his mouth upon her breasts. She wanted to hold him, be joined, and shatter with him.

She wanted him. It seemed almost decadent to be so clear about it, but she didn't lie to herself. She wanted him in the worst—no, make that the best—way.

And it wasn't as if he were running from the idea. He wanted to be with her just as much, but was resisting out of some sense of mistaken nobility.

As she lay there in the darkness, remembering the feel of his hands, his body, his mouth, she made up her mind. All her life, she'd been acted upon, instead of being the actor. Her daily runs were the first thing she'd ever initiated on her own, and in turn they'd given her the courage to initiate her bid to work in the prison kitchens, so she could be in a place where she could express her creativity.

That success had led to her decision to ask for visitation rights with Antonio when she was released, which led to her position here at the ranch.

Which led to Ramón.

And she wasn't going to fade passively into the background now, either. There was something deep and rich between her and Ramón, and she would always wonder what might have happened if she didn't act.

So tonight she donned a seductively elegant dress of black velvet, cocktail length, with cap sleeves that showed her lean arms, and a square neck that bared a good deal of chest. Not cleavage, because she lacked that particular commodity, but she thought the small swell of breast over the neckline was quite nice. She'd kept the boys in mind, of course, so it was only a little low-cut, just enough.

She left her hair loose, brushing her collarbone. Her stockings were sheer black, the shoes strappy little black sandals that showed off her slim ankles.

Stepping back to admire herself in the long mirror over her dresser, Tanya smiled. The reflection showed her a woman, strong and whole and fully grown—and for one tiny moment, she felt a shift in her awareness, as if she were part of all the women who'd ever claimed this power, as if they were all with her.

And when she came down the stairs, Ramón was standing by the fireplace in the living room, adjusting his bolero in the mirror over the mantel. He caught sight of her in the reflection, and froze, hands on his collar, then turned slowly to watch her descend. His liquid dark eyes were ablaze.

Tanya felt her stomach flip. Ramón, too, had dressed up. He wore a black shirt, cowboy cut with pearlized snaps, and close-fitting black jeans, and fancy black boots that made his legs look even longer. His hair, though it could never be entirely tamed, had been brushed back from his high forehead.

A wave of heat struck her, so fierce she wanted only to rip the clothes off him and make love right there. It didn't help that the same wish was in his face as his gaze moved over her, lingeringly, taking in the cut of the dress, the square bodice, her legs in the black stockings. His nostrils flared, and he met her at the foot of the stairs. He stood close, and looked at her, touched her shoulder with one finger. "Did you do this to torture me?"

"Yes." Up close, he smelled of after-shave and soap. "You smell good," she said.

He didn't move, just stood there, admiring her until Tanya felt almost uncomfortable. "Don't you think we should go on in? It's almost time for the buses to arrive."

"I can't move," he said, shaking his head. "I'm slain where I stand."

Tanya gave him a half grin and swung around. "Well, I can move." She headed down the hall, hearing him come behind, his boot heels sharp against the wooden floor. As they passed through the kitchen, Tanya gave Desmary a broad wink.

Ramón couldn't take his eyes off her all evening. As the kids filed in, spit-shined and shaved and buttoned, and the music started to play its pounding beat, he watched her from the corner of his eye. How could he hope to resist her now?

The dress was a killer. And he wasn't the only male in the room to notice. Dave was solicitous as she approached the punch table, and two of the other counselors stood alongside her as she drank it.

When had she become such a hot-looking woman? Always before, she was sweetly attractive. Or when she came out of prison, attractive with that hungry coyote edge. Now she looked like a well-groomed tigress, sleek and lean, her hair gleaming, her skin glowing. Her breasts, softly curved above the square bodice, invited the lingering eye, the caress of a tongue. . . .

He shifted uncomfortably, wondering if every boy in the room noticed, too. Probably not, actually. To them, Tanya was older than dirt.

Behind him, a soft voice said, "Shee! Lookit Ms. Bishop."

Maybe she wasn't so old. And the truth was, her dress was elegantly cut, very simple and attractive. It didn't show off more flesh than it should. It was just the way it fit her. Or maybe the way she moved.

Or maybe he just had it bad. She turned to put her glass on the table and her hair flowed away from her skin to clasp her face, leaving behind a bare, uncovered spot on her shoulder that was unbearably tender.

"Hey, Dad," Tonio said, next to him. "I want you to meet somebody."

Relieved at the distraction, Ramón turned.

Tonio, neat in a blue sweater that showed off his eyes, and a pair of creased khakis, held hands with a girl. "This is Teresa Guerro. Teresa, this is my dad, Mr. Quezada."

Small and neat, she lifted her shy gaze to his. She wasn't particularly beautiful, but Ramón saw instantly the quality that made Edwin and Tonio fight over her. There was a luminosity in her large dark eyes, an inviting curve to her full lips. "*Hola*, Mr. Quezada." In her words he heard the accent of a native Spanish speaker.

"Hello," Ramón said. "Tonio has told me a lot about you."

"He's talked a lot about you, too," she said, and gave Tonio a bright glance.

"Do you want to stand here with my dad for a minute while I get you some punch?" Tonio asked.

Teresa nodded. "Okay."

Which left Ramón needing to make small talk with a fourteen-year-old girl he didn't necessarily think was the best person in the world for his son. Tanya's black dress caught his eye, and he gestured for her to come over.

"So, are you from Manzanares, Teresa?" he asked. "I don't think I remember any Guerros from my days there."

"Umm, no. We just came here. We've been in Texas. But my mom wants me to finish high school in an American school." She blushed bright red. "I mean a New Mexico school."

Ramón smiled to reassure her he wouldn't pick up on her gaffe, but it told him what he needed to know about her family—and made sense of the fact Tonio said she was really smart, but not too good at schoolwork. "Is your mother a farm worker?"

Teresa nodded. "My dad, too, till he had a heart attack two years ago. It's been just me and my mom since then, but she got married this year."

"That's nice."

Tanya joined them, and Ramón introduced her. "Oh, Ms. Bishop!" Teresa said. "Tonio talks about you all the time."

"He does?" Tanya beamed. "I'm glad."

Carrying two cups of punch in clear plastic glasses, Tonio returned. He whistled at Tanya, who smiled and bowed mockingly. "Thank you, thank you."

The four of them made small talk for a minute or two, and a song came on, a loud rocking rap song. "Let's dance," Tonio said, grabbing Teresa's hand and heading toward the dance floor.

Tanya turned laughing eyes toward Ramón. "Can you dance to your precious rap?"

He smiled. "Sure. A-one an-a-two." Playfully, he danced an old-fashioned two-step.

She laughed. "That's about the only dancing I can do, too. Can't even do that very well, though I certainly did my best to learn."

"It's easy, baby," he said with an exaggerated leer. "Let me show you."

"Quit," Tanya said, holding him back just as mockingly with one hand. "You have to be a good example, remember?"

He leaned close, as if he would kiss her, and took a triumphant pleasure in the heated flare in her eyes. "If I weren't such an upstanding citizen, I might say to hell with providing examples."

"But you are upstanding."

"Very." He straightened his spine to illustrate.

She sipped the punch she held. "I haven't seen Edwin tonight."

"That's because he got suspended the same day he went back to school."

"Fighting again?"

"Smoking cigarettes in the boys' room."

Tanya frowned. "I could almost feel sorry for him. How does a child get so lost?"

"I don't know." He lifted a shoulder. "And sometimes, unfortunately, the only thing to do for them is just let them hit a wall. That's the only thing that will work for Edwin."

"Maybe."

Ramón scanned the room, keeping his eye open for trouble of any kind, or potential trouble. And spied a little. In one darkened corner, under the floating pumpkins and trailers of crepe paper, a boy and a girl were making out. "Excuse me. I have to break up Romeo and Juliet over there."

Tanya chuckled.

Putting his hand on her arm, Ramón said, "Save me a slow dance, eh?"

She gave him a slow, impossibly sexy smile. "You got it."

Tanya couldn't remember the last time she'd had so much fun. She got to call the numbers for the door prize tickets for movie and skating passes, and when the dance contest started, she was a judge. Everything about the night was just plain fun.

Zach, dressed up in a plaid shirt and jeans she had pressed for him, his hair wet-combed with a neat part, was her constant companion through the evening. She put him to work behind the punch bowl, filling glasses with a big ladle, and let him help her bring out fresh crudités when the first batch ran out. She dragged him out on the dance floor at one point and teasingly taught him the box-step, and although he blushed furiously and clung to her hand so tightly she thought he'd crack her fingers, he managed to last an entire song.

After that, she found herself dancing a lot. She cheerfully declined the fast songs, but danced with counselors and some of the other boys who were too young to have asked dates.

She was gulping a drink of water when Tonio appeared at her side. The DJ had put on some Spanish songs, to the sound of groans and protests from some of the boys, and cheers from the others. Tonio grinned. "Can you dance to this music?"

She grinned. "This is how I learned to dance—at VFW dances with—" A cool wash of realization touched her. She'd almost said, "your dad," but amended it to, "my ex-husband."

Politely, he gestured toward the open floor. "Will you dance with me?"

Startled, Tanya looked toward Ramón, who stood watching from the other side of the room. He smiled at her and nodded once. Tanya put her glass on the table. "It's been a while," she said with a lift of her eyebrows, "but if you don't mind a bruised toe, sure."

They walked onto the floor. Tonio turned and held out his hands. She put her left hand on his shoulder, her right hand into his and looked up. He smiled, paused a moment to find the beat, and they started to dance.

Tanya's heart caught, hard. As the music swirled around them, she thought about all the years she'd waited to see him, trying to imagine how he looked or talked. Now she danced with him, and could smell the clean scent of his soap, could see the way his hair grew from a widow's peak on his forehead, and his strong white teeth when he grinned down at her encouragingly. "You're good at this."

"Thanks." To stem the huge well of joyful emotion rising in her throat, she forced herself to empty her mind. Some moments in life were too beautiful to hold at once. She would have to let it all flow into her and look it over again later.

The song was a familiar ballad of love lost, as so many Spanish ballads seemed to be. "Sad song."

"Can you understand it?"

She nodded.

"You used to be married?"

Tanya looked up. "Yes, a long time ago."

"To a Spanish guy?"

Dangerous territory, this. She tripped and righted herself. "Sorry," she said, looking down at her feet in the strappy sandals. "Yes."

"You don't like to talk about it, huh?"

Relieved she raised her head. "No. It was a long time ago."

"I understand."

To change the subject, she said, "Are you having a good time tonight?"

"Yeah, I am. It was the right thing to do, writing that letter."

"I guess it was. She seems very nice."

"She is." He glanced over his shoulder to where she sat by the table, rubbing one foot. "She had to borrow the shoes from her mom. Her feet hurt her when we dance."

"Poor thing."

He nodded, his face going soft. "I like her a lot."

The song ended, and Tanya let go. "You're a good dancer," she said, clasping her hands together. "Thank you."

With a small bow, he smiled. "No, thank you. All the guys will be jealous that Ms. Bishop danced with me."

She laughed.

Ramón came up beside them. "Trying to steal my girl, eh?" he said to Tonio, feinting a punch to his upper arm.

"Yeah."

"My turn," Ramón said, taking Tanya's hand. "Excuse us," he said to Tonio.

Tonio grinned and ambled off the cleared area to sit down next to Teresa. The next song started, a mournful, slow song. Only a few couples danced. The rest were milling around, picking up coats and having one last drink of punch or stack of cookies before the danced ended at eleven.

"Finally," Ramón said, taking her into his arms. His embrace was light, leaving a respectful pillow of air between them. He looked down at her, and stepped infinitesimally closer. "I've been waiting for this all evening."

"Me, too," Tanya said, huskily.

Their forearms met in a close press, and his arm around her waist drew her near. The expression in his dark eyes was thick with desire. "I've been trying so hard not to think about you as my lover," he said very quietly, expertly leading her in the familiar steps. "But I can't stop."

She looked at his mouth, so close to her own, and edged slightly closer still, until their chests met in barest contact. Somehow their legs slipped into a woven pattern, and along the inside of her knee, Tanya felt the brush of his pant leg. "Don't stop then," she said, raising her eyes to his. "I know I haven't."

He sighed and his fingers skimmed her back. "I want you," he said. "They don't have to know."

"No one needs to know."

His thumb moved on her palm in a circle. "Do you want me, Tanya?"

"Yes," she whispered, and felt her knees brush his, her thighs against his thighs, her breasts against his chest. "Yes, I do. I want to kiss you and touch you and make love with you."

His mouth lifted in a wry, half smile. "I still have a whole box of condoms."

Tanya grinned. "Good. You might need them."

"All of them?"

"You never know."

He glanced around the room, but no one was watching them. Subtly, he pressed himself against her, and Tanya pressed back, thrilling to the evidence of his desire. They swayed in the dance, hips moving back and forth, and Ramón sighed against her ear.

"I can't wait to taste you," he whispered against her ear. His tongue snaked out and touched her earlobe. Tanya shivered against him, a low throb starting to ache in her nether regions. His voice was hoarse and quiet and low-pitched. "I'm going to unzip this dress very, very slowly." His fingers moved on the zipper. "And I'm going to kiss every inch of your back, and then your arms. And then your breasts."

"Mmm." She closed her eyes, trying desperately to remain normal-looking.

"I'm going to suckle your breasts and kiss your tummy and—"

"Stop," she whispered. "I'm going to melt right here."

"Good," he replied.

She pulled back to look at him. "Not good. Behave yourself, Mr. Quezada."

He grinned, wickedly, and she felt everything in her body go soft. "Do you really want me to?"

A crash and a scream rent the air. Tanya whirled and heard Ramón cry, "No, Edwin!" He broke free, and before Tanya had completed turning around, he was halfway across the room. "Edwin!" he bellowed.

Tanya could not immediately see what happened. A knot of chaos erupted all around her. Kids scurried here and there, away from the trouble, which centered around the place Tonio and Teresa had been sitting moments before. Another scream—a yelp, really—rang out.

Then she saw Edwin, holding Teresa, dragging her toward the door. She wore only one shoe, and her limping up and down gait caused her to stumble. Edwin yanked her up and she cried out, sobbing, trying to wrench herself free. Tanya couldn't see Tonio. Where was he?

Before she knew what she was doing, Tanya had kicked off her shoes and started toward them, some primal feeling in her chest. She walked, measuring the distance between the kitchen door—his only way out—and herself and him. Counselors herded other kids toward the edges of the room, and Tanya finally spied Tonio, flat on the floor, a mark on his forehead. He looked dazed as he got to his knees.

She looked back at Edwin—and finally saw what made the others stay back. He had a knife. Not just any old knife, but a big, ultrasharp knife with a black handle they used for cutting meat with bones—like chicken.

Like flesh.

In a blaze of confusion, she wondered how he'd gotten hold of it, for all knives were carefully locked in a cabinet at night. But he'd had KP for weeks and must have secreted it away.

Teresa stumbled again, and Edwin grabbed her by the waist, holding the knife close to her face. The wild menace in his face, the animal bloodlust in his eyes sent loathing and fear through Tanya. She'd seen that look, that mindlessness. Her heart pounded. The sound was loud and fast and hard in her ears, and still she edged toward the kitchen door.

Ramón walked close to them, and Edwin made a grunting noise, warning him away. Ramón lifted his hands, palms out, in the same gesture he'd used with Tanya the first day in the bus station. "Let her go,

Edwin. You won't get anywhere with her. And all you're doing is digging yourself a deeper hole."

Edwin edged along the wall, holding the girl hard next to him. She wept soundlessly, frozen, her hands on Edwin's arm, her eyes on the knife.

At the expression on her face, something in Tanya's gut twisted. Anger, as clear and white and hot as the desert sun, filled her. Not again. Not another one.

He was only a few feet away, his eyes on Ramón, who continued to advance. Tanya lunged. Her legs were strong with her running, her arms filled with muscle from her work in the kitchen. She had surprise on her side. She seized Edwin's wrist and kicked him squarely where it would do the most damage. He grunted and doubled over, dropping the knife. Teresa sobbed and pulled free.

Ramón grabbed the knife and looked over his shoulder. Already sirens sounded in the distance, and Tanya realized vaguely that someone must have already called the police.

Her breath came fast, still riding the wild emotion pumping through her chest. She squatted in front of Edwin. "Don't you ever hurt another woman again. Not ever."

With a snarl, he lifted his head and glared at her. He uttered a foul epithet about the evil nature of women.

Tanya smiled tightly. "You got it."

Chapter Thirteen

Dear Antonio,
I'm aching for a normal life. Everyday life. People and ordinary arguments and dust on lamp shades. I'm aching to live in a place with curtains on the windows, and a place where you don't have to hide everything that crosses your mind.

I don't let myself think much beyond that, but it would be so great to have babies again one of these days. It's really the one thing I wanted, even when I was a little girl—to grow up and have babies of my own. I like children a lot, little ones and big ones both, girls and boys. I liked being pregnant and my labor was easy, and it seemed the most natural thing in the world for me. Like when I was made, the angels looked in their little bag and said, "I think we'll make this one a mother," then gave me everything I'd need for it. Like my friend Iris, who is an artist. She sees color in a different way than the rest of us— each tiny hue and variation means something to her. Speaks to her. She takes those color voices and puts them on a canvas or a piece of paper, and makes everyone else hear the voices, too.

That's how it is with me and mothering. I know, in my deepest heart, that was what I was supposed to do. And though I'm your mother, and I got to have some time with you, and there's always going to be a special link between us, I haven't really been able to be your mother all these years. I bet your voice is changing now— you'll be more than half-grown by the time they let me out.

But maybe I'll get to do a little more mothering with you, or maybe you'll have my grandchildren and I can do it that way. Somehow, I have to believe that.

Love, Mom

Reaction set in later. As the police cuffed Edwin and took him to town, Tanya felt telltale trembling fill her limbs. Nausea rose in her stomach. Dizzy and sick, she went to the kitchen and concentrated on making a cup of tea.

As she sat down to drink it, Zach appeared. His little face was pale and stark. "Hi, honey," Tanya said, extending a hand to draw him into the kitchen. "You want to come sit in my lap for a minute?"

He looked over his shoulder, as if afraid there would be some older boy to make fun of him if he admitted to still wanting such things.

"I need a hug," Tanya said. "That kind of scared me. Did it scare you?"

His expression eased, and he nodded, moving forward. Tanya moved back from the table to make room on her lap, and Zach eased his skinny body gingerly onto her legs. She rubbed his back. "Everything is okay now."

"I'm glad they arrested him. He was mean to me."

"He was? Did you tell anybody?"

Zach sighed and shook his head. She kept rubbing his back. "I was afraid he'd be meaner if I did."

"Oh, honey." She pulled him close. He wasn't a very large child and still fit neatly in her lap.

Almost as if against his will, he put his head on her shoulder and started to cry. "I was scared for you," he said, and suddenly put his arms around her very tightly.

"Go ahead and cry it out, sweetie. Don't believe all those people who say it doesn't help anything—it helps a lot."

"What if he had hurt you bad? Or cut your throat?"

"He didn't. I'm okay. I'm sorry you were frightened, Zach, I really am. If I'd thought for a minute..." What? She wouldn't have acted? That wasn't true. "He didn't," she repeated.

He fell silent against her, his tears drying quickly. He made no immediate move to get away, however, so Tanya relaxed, her arms around his painfully thin body. "It's nice to hold a boy again," she said after a little while. "I used to have a little boy, did I tell you that?"

Zach shook his head. "Did he die, like my mom?"

"No." Tanya sighed. "No, thank goodness. I lost him, that's all. Maybe I'll tell you about it someday." She began to rock slowly, back and forth, and began to hum. "I used to hold him and sing to him. Can I sing you a song?"

"I think I'm too big for a song."

"Who's going to know?" She felt him smile against her neck, and from the weight of his body slumped against hers, he was getting sleepy. "Even grown-up boys listen to music sometimes when they've had a bad day."

He yawned. "Okay."

Tanya hummed quietly through the song to get her voice, then very quietly, she began to sing Tonio's song to him. By the time she reached the end, Zach was slumped and snoring softly. A movement at the door caught her eye, and she looked up to see Tonio standing there, a strange expression on his face. A cool sense of shock washed through her—her guard was slipping fast. To cover her feelings of guilt, she smiled. "He's out cold."

Tonio nodded and came into the room. "I'll take him and put him to bed."

"Thanks." Tanya stood and shifted the weight of Zach into Tonio's waiting arms. She smiled. "You're really a good kid, you know it?"

He smiled, but said nothing.

With a sigh, Tanya sat back down at her tea, gone lukewarm now. She covered her face with her hands, dizzy with everything that had happened—not only tonight, but since she'd been released from prison. Her life had changed so much!

That was where Ramón found her, sitting at the kitchen table, mug between her cold hands. He looked grim. The scuffle had mussed his carefully tamed hair, and it had sprung into its natural, wild waves over his head. She thought she understood why he wore it longer than normal—cut short, it would be uncontrollable. He touched the bridge of his nose. "That was crazy, Tanya."

She winced. "I know. I didn't do it with a lot of conscious thought. I just saw the chance and..." She let the words trail off and raised her hand.

With a sigh, he sank into the chair opposite. "It was brave, too."

She said nothing, only looked at her hands.

"*I* wanted to be the hero, you know." There was teasing in his voice. "That's how it's supposed to be. The guy does the heroic stuff, the girl squeals on the sidelines.

Tanya looked up and saw his wry smile. "Sorry. I'll practice my squealing for next time."

"Let's hope there is no next time."

"There will be." She sucked in a breath of air and let it go on a sigh. "There always is."

From the dining room came the sounds of cleanup. Tonio came in. A smear of dust marked his dark blue shirt, and there was a goose egg on his forehead. "Zach's safely in bed," he said.

"You okay?" Ramón asked.

"Yeah." He looked down. "But Teresa's mom is pretty upset."

"I can understand that."

"He took me by surprise." He touched the goose egg gingerly. "I don't even know what he hit me with."

"A plain old rock," Ramón said. "It's in there by the chair where you fell."

"Jeez." His head was bowed, but he lifted it now and looked at Tanya. "Where'd you learn to fight, lady?"

"Long story. I'll tell it to you someday."

He nodded slowly. "I'm going to bed. Good night, you guys." He ambled out of the kitchen, into the main part of the house, leaving a deep silence behind him.

Tanya stared at her tea, watching the lights play over the surface in rippling waves. "We have to tell him," she said.

"Yes, we do."

"How do you think he'll take it?"

Ramón sucked his teeth, shook his head. "I really don't have any idea, Tanya. You takes yer cards and plays yer hand."

She nodded. In the dining room, a pair of voices quieted with the slam of a door, and there was silence.

"At last," Ramón said, and rubbed his face. He looked at her. "Come here, will you?"

Her heart jumped, and without knowing she would, she got up and moved around the table to his side. He took her hand and tugged her into his lap. As she put her arms around his neck and rested her head on his shoulder, pounds of tension drained suddenly from her body. He, too, sighed, as if he'd needed her closeness to ease him.

He held her loosely, his cheek against her hair, his hands joined around her waist. Tanya closed her eyes at the comfort of his touch, and breathed of his scent—faint traces of after-shave and shampoo, and deeper, the notes of his very flesh, redolent of the desert and its secrets. She shifted and pressed her forehead and the bridge of her nose against his neck.

Gently he rubbed her back, smoothing his hand over her hip, back to her waist. A strange, unfamiliar feeling crept through her, calm and sweet, so comforting she didn't recognize it at first.

Trust.

It was such a strange feeling, she raised her head to look at him. He met her gaze evenly, his fathomless eyes promising honor and gentleness. She could touch him her way, explore him according to her needs—and his, too, of course—but he'd be patient while she learned him.

Earlier, she'd wanted him, with her body and a certain yearning incompleteness she didn't know how to name. Now a bone-deep need grew in her, a need to love him and let him love her in return, a need to show him she trusted him as she'd trusted no other, a need to—

He touched her face, and his long fingers spread wide to cup her jaw, her cheekbone, her temple, and his eyes were intent on her mouth. She kissed him, or he kissed her, and there was a sighing, breathy sound that came from them both. "Ah, Tanya," he said, and pulled her closer.

They kissed for a long time, and Tanya touched him, his hair and his ears and his throat where his blood ran under the skin. He stroked her back and rubbed his open palm over her thigh, and skimmed his hand under her skirt, over the slippery stockings. They parted ever so slightly, breath mingling. "I think we should go upstairs," he said.

"Yes."

And it was so easy to stand up and let him take her hand, and go through the house, turning off lights. He paused at the foot of the stairs to kiss her, as if he were nibbling something addictive. "Mmm," he said, and took her hand again, smiling.

They stopped by his room, quietly. He took the box of condoms out of a drawer and dropped them in the pocket of his robe, which he also carried with him. Tanya watched from the doorway, leaning against the doorjamb, admiring him. His movements were fluid and easy, and she liked how he handled the things he needed to bring without embarrassment. Open. He hid nothing, so he had no fear of exposure.

When he turned off the lamp by the bed, he came to her and put his hands on either side of her face, pressing his body along the length of her, and kissed her again, long and deep, as if he could never taste it enough.

Tanya smiled up at him. "You're so...wonderful," she said, and blushed because it sounded so silly.

He dipped, smiling, and touched his tongue to her lips. "Just wait."

And seized with a sudden silliness, they raced up the rest of the stairs to Tanya's room, hissing for the other to be quiet, tripping on the tie of his robe, and each other. At last they were safely inside her room, and the door was closed, and they fell on each other.

Ramón dropped his robe on the floor and reached for her at the same moment she reached for him. She tugged open the snaps on his shirt, until his brown, bare chest was exposed to her hands and her mouth. Ramón unzipped her dress, and slipped his hands underneath the fabric. She felt her bra give way, as he unfastened the hook, and she skimmed his shirt off his shoulders. He let her push it off his arms, leaving his torso bare, then took her dress and bra from her shoulders and helped them fall to the floor. He bent to gather her close, to kiss her, and Tanya gasped at the electric sensation of his naked chest against her breasts.

He breathed her name, and his kiss grew fierce. For one instant, he let her go, and knelt to take the box from his robe pocket, then walked her backward to the bed, until the back of her knees bumped the mattress. They tumbled down together, kicking off their shoes, skimming off jeans and stockings, kissing and kissing and kissing. Ramón played her body like a fiddle, setting it to a furious, building tune, using his hands, his mouth, his limbs, to tease and tantalize and arouse.

At last, gasping with need, she grabbed his shoulders. "I want you inside me, Ramón, before I die of needing you."

"Yes." He reached for the box, flipping the lid with his thumb and dumping the contents in their slippery foil packs on the bed. Tanya grabbed one and tore the foil with her teeth and took the condom out. She paused.

"I haven't made love to anyone since Victor," she said. "We don't have to do this."

"Yes, we do." He reached for it, but Tanya moved her hand away.

She smiled. "Allow me, *señor*."

He lifted a little to give her access, and groaned as her fingers slid over the length of him. Tanya moved, and he put himself between her thighs. For a moment he paused. "I've wanted this for more years than I can count," he whispered, and kissed her breast, then her mouth. Tanya ached, feeling him at her nethermost. His hair brushed her lips as he kissed her throat, and the sensation was erotic, tantalizing.

"Ramón," she whispered. "Come *home*."

He let go of a ragged chuckle, and she could tell by his breathing it was not so easy for him to stay so torturously poised, either. "You sure?" He kissed her gently, bracing himself on his arms. "We won't be the same after this, not you or me, or us."

"I'm sure." She put her hands on his firm buttocks and lifted her hips, and there was no more teasing from him. He made a low pleasured sound and eased into her. Tanya heard her own moan roll into the room—it was so right! She sighed his name, her hands moving on his back and hips, and the backs of his thighs. She arched. "Ramón!"

He gathered her close and drove home and there was no thought, only wide bands of feelings, only touching as they tangled hands and mouths and legs, as they rocked in ancient rhythm. Tanya felt him all through her, all around her, and he was right—it was like nothing she'd ever known. The way they melded, the way each cry, each kiss, each small movement increased the joining until there was only one being, not two. One soul, one mind, one heart, irretrievably entwined.

Ramón kissed her and Tanya tumbled, her body pulsing around his. She cried out in a sobbing voice against his lips and heard him whisper, "Sweet, sweet Tanya." He rocked her harder, closer, his lips and movements intense and wild and so vividly pleasurable Tanya thought she could happily die.

And then his mouth was all over her face and her neck and his hands held her close and she felt him come apart, throbbing within her.

He buried his face against her neck, slowly moving, letting the waves slow in him, in her. There was sweat between their chests, and their pounding, racing hearts beat only millimeters apart. Their breath tangled in the darkness. Tanya lifted her hands from his back and touched his head, putting her fingers in that silky, springy hair. She turned her head and kissed his ear, filled with emotions too broad, too intense, too new to name. Ramón planted tiny kisses on her collarbone, her throat, her chin.

They shifted to lie side by side, and tugged the covers over them. Tanya touched his face, suddenly overwhelmed with the fact that it was Ramón here in her arms. She kissed his forehead, between his eyes, and his nose. "I'm in love with you, Ramón," she whispered, touching his jaw, his mouth.

"Don't say it," he said, and kissed her, as if to blot out the words. "You owe me nothing."

Smelling the scent of their joining, together with the notes of his skin, Tanya thought: I owe you everything, but she didn't say it. She contented herself with the feel of him warm against her and the joy of being in complete union with another human for possibly the first time in her life.

They dozed and woke up starving. Ramón tiptoed downstairs and brought back a big plate of leftovers from the party, along with cans of grape soda. When he came back into her room, he stopped just inside the door, closed his eyes, and opened them again. It wasn't a dream. Tanya, sensual as a cat, waited for him in bed, naked beneath the green sheets and blankets of her bed. Her dark golden hair tumbled in disarray around her face, and one lean bare arm held the sheets to her breasts. She was beautiful, delectable, everything he'd ever wanted. Emotion slammed him, so strong and intense, he knew he was lost.

Settling the food on the lamp table beside the bed, Ramón sat down. "Hi," he said, holding out a carrot stick.

"Hi." She chomped the carrot right from his fingers and leaned back. "Come here often?"

"Not recently." He lifted a wicked brow. "Perhaps I could be persuaded with the right incentives."

"Ah, what incentives could those be?"

He grabbed the cover and tugged it down to show one round, pink-tipped breast. He closed his mouth over the nub, moving his tongue over the eager pearling, and heard her sigh. "This is pretty tasty," he said.

"All yours." She tugged him by the hair to her mouth so she could kiss him, hard.

Ramón chuckled against her lips, moving his hand against her belly. "You know how many times I hear that in a day?"

She pulled his robe open and curled her hand around him. "It's a tough life."

"Yes, it is." He kissed her and she moved her hands on him, and Ramón felt awash on her, in their passion. At one point, he took her face in his hands and just looked at her. She opened her long, exotic blue eyes and he saw the stars there, the happiness that had been so long absent, and a physical pain touched him. Slowly, deliberately, he put his lips to hers. So in love, he thought. So in love.

But he didn't say it. He only showed her again with the most ancient of movements, the most powerful of body language.

Just before dawn, her alarm went off. Tanya moved to hit the snooze button, then turned back to Ramón, who seemed not to hear it. His heat and satin and scent of desert morning struck her forcibly, and an impossible tingling roved over her nerves. In the stillness she curled up to him, nestling her head against his arm, putting her hand on his flat belly.

Her body sang. In the pale gray light, she propped her head on her arms and watched him sleep. His face was almost unbearably handsome in sleep, his mouth full and commanding, so exotically his own. And she liked his nose, that high-bridged conquistador's nose with the elegantly shaped nostrils that flared so tellingly when he was aroused or angry.

She liked the way his hair sprang back from his forehead, defiant and wild, and liked the forehead itself, for it was high and strong and very intelligent.

She liked him—the way he moved and talked. The way he could make an entire room of surly teenage boys jump to attention with a single, hawkish lift of one brow. She liked the way he made an old woman giggle, and the devotion he inspired in the animals. A good man.

He stirred. Wickedly, Tanya took the covers off him so she could admire all of him. He shifted ever so slightly, and she put her hand on his thigh, long and lean, then his knee which was not, she had to admit, the most beautiful she'd ever seen. She moved back up and touched his dark nipples with her tongue, and then leaned over him, her breasts pressing into his arm, to kiss his throat.

Below her, he stirred, but Tanya continued to tease him awake, fluttering her hands over his manhood, over the thin line of hair on his belly and around the circle of his navel. She kissed his earlobe and stayed to suckle there.

And then he was making love to her again, his body hot on hers, in hers.

Afterward, sated once more, they lay in each other's arms. "I want to tell Tonio who I am," Tanya said. "It's important."

"Give it a day or two, huh?"

"What difference will it make?"

His eyes were grim. "We don't really know how he'll react."

"It's better than keeping up this lie, Ramón. It was okay at first, but I think he's already guessed. You and I will look a lot better in his eyes if we confess before he confronts one of us."

Ramón shifted his head on the pillow and rubbed a circle around her hip. "If he doesn't react well, you'll have to leave the ranch."

Tanya nodded.

"Let's just play it by ear, okay?" Ramón said. "There's been a lot going on the past week or two. Tonio probably doesn't need any more complications."

She sighed. "I don't like the lying."

"I know." He sighed, loudly. "You know, I'm being purely selfish. I don't want to deal with it yet, and that's the real problem."

"I'll wait a day or two, then, if you want me to."

He kissed her. "I want." As if to underscore the comment, his stomach growled, loudly. They both laughed. "Time to get up, I guess."

Tanya stretched, watching him lazily as he pulled on his robe. His body was sinewy, his flesh the color of the burnt sienna crayon she'd loved as a child. He saw her watching him and winked. "I'll see you downstairs." He bent over her in the bed and kissed her mouth, then the swell of a breast. "Mmm."

She chuckled. "Okay. I have to get moving, too, but I just want one more minute."

"Better hurry—it's almost light."

"I will."

"Same time, same place tonight?" he asked wickedly.

"Yes, please."

He winked and left her. Tanya sighed happily. This morning, life was exactly what it should be all the time. Heaven. Sheer heaven. She wouldn't think of Tonio just yet. There was time. What difference could a day or two make?

Chapter Fourteen

Dear Antonio,
This is the last letter I will have to write to you.
Tomorrow, at 10:00 a.m., I will be free of the
New Mexico penal system. They've even waived
parole because my record is so clean, and because I've shown myself able to handle the world
by living in a halfway house for the past year. It's
almost normal life, the halfway house. Not
quite, but enough. I know I'm ready to put this
chapter behind me and go forward.

Ramón has hired me at the ranch, and we've
decided it would be best for me to ease into your
life. He says you feel betrayed, and though it

hurts me, I guess I understand. I was so young and broken by the time Victor's family came after me that I just let you go. I meant to keep you safe, *hijo*. That's all. I hope you'll understand that one of these days.

In the meantime, I get to actually put my eyes on you again, after more than four thousand days of waiting. Such sweetness is rare.

We survived, you and I. That's a lot.

Love, Mom

When Ramón came downstairs after a shower, even his skin tingled with afterglow. Whistling, he took the last turn in the stairs and headed for the kitchen, wondering how in the world he'd keep a straight face when he looked at Tanya. How could anyone look at either one of them and not see the newly bloomed love between them?

A noise in his office halted him and he doubled back to push open the door. Tonio sat in his office chair, a folder open in his hand. A file drawer gaped open—the personnel files. Ramón didn't have to guess which folder Tonio held.

Tonio didn't even startle as Ramón came in. He looked up miserably, tears streaming down his face. "How could you?" he asked, and it wasn't the sulky challenge of a selfish teenager, but the agonized whisper of betrayal.

"Damn," Ramón said, stepping into the room. "Don't jump to conclusions here, Tonio. Give me a chance to explain."

"Explain what? That you lied? That you brought my mother here without telling me and pretended she was somebody else all this time?" He threw the file at Ramón's feet. Tears still washed over the almost manly cheeks, and his eyes held a terrible light.

Ramón didn't move for a moment. "Don't blame Tanya. She's been wanting to tell you for weeks."

"And you stopped her? Why?"

And Ramón knew, just that quickly, that he'd been wrong. "I don't know," he said. "I'm sorry."

"She killed my father! How can you forgive her for that?"

"It isn't that simple, Tonio." He reached for him— and Tonio bolted away, as if in revulsion. Ramón halted, pursed his lips for a moment, thinking, trying to remember what it was like to be fourteen and morally outraged. "Read the whole file."

"No!" His eyes slitted. "I want her to leave. I don't want to see her."

"You're making a mistake, Antonio."

The boy abruptly sat down again and put his head in his hands. A sob, all the more painful for the manly rasp it held, broke from his chest. "How could you play such an awful trick on me?"

Ramón went to him and embraced him, pulling his head into the hollow of his shoulder. "It wasn't meant to be a trick, Tonio. I swear. I wanted you to get to know her slowly, so you wouldn't feel put upon to be nice if you didn't want to. It made a lot of sense at the time. I'm sorry. I was wrong."

A sound at the door drew his attention. Father and son both raised their heads and saw Tanya standing in the doorway, a stricken expression on her face. "It was the song, wasn't it?" she said quietly. Ramón saw her knuckles were white where she clung to the door. "You heard me singing that song to Zach last night."

Tonio jumped to his feet, and Ramón grabbed him, hard. "You gave me away!" Tonio cried, jerking hard at Ramón's hold on him.

Tanya nodded. Ramón saw her dark blue eyes fill with tears. But as she stood there, it was as if a straight line pulled her upright. She lifted her chin and met Tonio's accusatory glare. "Yes," she said, simply. "I had to."

"I hate you! Both of you!" Tonio cried, and he tore free of Ramón's grip. He bolted toward the door.

Tanya stepped out of his way. "I'm sorry, Antonio," she said quietly.

With a sound of disgust, Tonio brushed by her. They heard his heavy feet on the stairs.

Tanya took a breath and looked at Ramón. "I'll pack now. You can take me to town to find a place after breakfast."

"He'll come around."

"Maybe." Her eyes were sad. "I'm not sure I would, in his shoes."

Unable to move, Ramón only nodded. Forced to choose between the two of them, he had to choose his child. "He will," Ramón repeated.

Tanya didn't reply—she just turned around and went up the stairs.

In the quiet left behind, Ramón squatted to pick up the file Tonio had flung at him. A picture of Tanya from prison was stapled to the inside. Her features looked hard, her mouth pinched, and he realized how much she'd changed since her arrival. He moved his finger over the photo. Damn.

It didn't take Tanya very long to gather her things. Even with the new things she'd purchased with her paycheck, everything she had fit into the prison-issue suitcase the state had given her. As she packed, the tortoiseshell cat played with her things, jumping into the suitcase, then out, then in. "Come on, Snoopy, get," Tanya said, finally exasperated. She picked up the cat and held him close. His fur smelled faintly of cinnamon and sunshine, and Tanya knew Desmary had been holding the cat sometime this morning, too. It gave her an unexpected burst of homesickness.

She loved the ranch! She loved working with the boys, loved cooking with Desmary, loved her room with it's high view and beautiful curtains. She loved running in the morning across the desert, and sitting at the supper table with Tonio and Ramón.

A piercing ache moved through her. Tonio. She'd been dreading this very thing, and now there was nothing to be done but clean up the pieces. She most adamantly did not want to leave the presence of her son, not after so long a time of not seeing him, but there was no choice. At least now he knew. She could live in Manzanares and work there, and be close to him, anyway.

Close to both of them.

She would miss every tiny little thing there was about this place. In a few short weeks, it had become her home more fully than any place she'd ever lived. She wished she could let her roots settle here, grow long and deep in the sandy soil. In time, she might even have learned to pluck a chicken.

Against the ache in her heart, she placed practicality. Sometimes things didn't work out the way you wanted, but you didn't stop living because of it. She had her freedom, and the dignity of knowing she had an honest trade to offer the world. Perhaps one of the cafés in town would hire her.

However all this ended, the Last Chance Ranch had truly given her a fair chance at life, renewing her resolve and determination, giving her a chance to love herself again. In doing so, she'd reclaimed the dignity that had been lost so long ago. Whatever else happened, that was worth coming here.

From the bottom drawer of the dresser, she took a stack of letters tied with string. Each was in an envelope, just as if she were going to mail it—but of course, she hadn't. She'd only written them, and put them away. And now she'd give them to the boy for whom they'd been intended. It was all she had to give him. The only way he'd understand.

Firmly, she closed the suitcase, made her bed, and then marched downstairs, her chin up. At the very least, she'd go with dignity. Ramón, looking bleak, took the letters from her as if accepting a sacred trust. "I'll see that he gets them," he said. His voice was raw.

In town, he saw her settled into the single decent hotel, over the diner, and paid her bill for a week, then walked upstairs with her. "I can manage from here," Tanya said, taking the key from him in the hall.

He watched her open the door, and set her suitcase just inside in the foyer. "I hate this," he said.

Tanya clenched her teeth, willing herself to be as calm as she could be, but waves of lonely protest washed through her as she stood there. "Me, too."

"Damn," he said, and pulled her close. "Maybe it won't be long."

She closed her eyes, smelling the tang of autumn in his jacket. His hair touched her forehead. For one long, indulgent moment, Tanya allowed herself to glory in his touch, in the wonder that was Ramón. She loved him. Deeply. And there was nothing she could do about it. She had chosen him to raise Antonio because she'd known he would put Antonio's welfare above everything else, as any good parent would do. Now she could hardly cry foul when he was doing exactly that.

"I wish things were different," she whispered. "I wish we'd told him the truth from the beginning."

Ramón pulled back and held her by her arms. "No, you don't. He would never have spoken to you, Tanya. Not one word. You have to trust me that we did the right thing."

She nodded. Plucking at his coat, she said, "You'd better get back."

"Are you sure you're all right?"

"I'm fine."

He gave her another quick hug, and pressed a kiss to her forehead. Then, as if he didn't trust himself, he hurried away. Tanya watched until the top of his head disappeared down the stairs.

After a subdued supper through which Tonio didn't speak one word unless he was spoken to first, Ramón called the boy into his office and gave him the letters.

"What is this?"

"Tanya . . . your mother wrote them from prison. To you."

Tonio tossed the packet back on Ramón's desk. "I don't want them."

Grimly, Ramón picked them up and lifted Tonio's hand and put the two together. "They're all you have—your only legacy."

Tonio stared at him, unmoving, and the dark blue stillness reminded Ramón deeply of Tanya. "What am I supposed to do with them?"

"How about read them?"

"No."

"Damn, Tonio, don't be so hard." He shook his head. "I've tried to never say anything too bad about Victor, your father, but it's time you really understood the truth."

"Don't bring him into it."

"I have to, Antonio." He stood up and walked to the window, where he stared at the night beyond. "He was mean, Tonio. Meaner than Edwin by a long shot. He was insanely jealous about your mother, too. She couldn't even talk to anyone else. When she finally left him because of his cruelty, he stalked her, over and over again. You know some of this, but I don't think you've given it enough thought."

There was suspicious moisture in Tonio's eyes again, and he blinked hard, finally looking down to the packet in his hands. "I don't remember either one of them," he said. "I just remember shouting. Screaming. My mother's long blond hair."

"You're old enough to know now, Antonio," Ramón said, turning to face him.

The boy's mouth was tight. "I don't want to know."

"It won't go away, son. Better to face it and get it over with now. You take those letters and read them."

"None of this little speech changes the fact that you lied to me."

"You're right." He crossed his arms. "But let's be real honest with ourselves, eh? When I got the first letter from her, asking if she could see you when she got out, you'd just spent an afternoon with your Tía Luna, and she spent the whole time poisoning your mind against your mother. Your father's family always did that. They hate your mother. If I'd brought Tanya in here and introduced her as your mother, you would have spit on her feet and refused to try to learn anything about her."

Tonio said nothing, just rubbed a thumb over the edge of the letters.

"You know I'm right, Tonio. You just don't want to admit there might be a reason to bend the rules once in a while. I practice honesty with you as much as I can, but you don't necessarily need to know everything."

Begrudgingly, Tonio nodded.

"You can go now, if you want," Ramón said. "Unless you want to play a round of chess or something."

"No, thanks." Tonio tapped the letters with his fingers, and Ramón knew he'd won. At least Tonio would read them. At least he'd know the truth. That was a lot more than most people got.

Chapter Fifteen

Dear Antonio,

It's my birthday today. I'm twenty-two. We went to McDonald's for a Happy Meal, then I took you to a movie—Bambi, out for a special showing. I hope you remember seeing it. It's a good movie. One I've always liked, even if the part about the mother is sad.

When we got home, I found all my china plates smashed to bits, and I know Victor, your father, has been here, and that he will be back. I don't know what will happen, but I want you to have this, so you know how much I love you, how special you are. Of all the things that have happened to me, you're the best.

I remember the night you were born. It was already midnight. You just barely made it on the tenth, eight minutes before the day changed. There had been so much noise and activity, but then everyone left. All the nurses and doctors and Victor and his family. And it was just you and I. They wanted to give you a bottle because you were so big they said my milk wouldn't be enough, but one kind nurse left you with me and said it wouldn't hurt anything if I nursed you, that if you were hungry later, they could always give you a bottle then.

So there we were in that quiet room that had been so loud, just you and me. You curled your fist and put it on my breast as you nursed and looked at me with those big, big eyes. Even then you had the longest eyelashes I'd ever seen, and a thick head of hair that was still wet from being inside of me. There was this big fat lump in my chest right then, like nothing could ever go wrong again, not as long as you were my child. And just as I thought that, you let go of nursing and took a great big breath and sighed, like you felt that way, too.

Tonight, you're going to go to the baby-sitter because I'm afraid of what's going to happen here. I can't stand to let you be so afraid again, like you were last time—screaming and screaming in your room. No. No, that's not going to

happen anymore. And maybe I won't be there to
give you hugs and kisses in person, so I'm giving them to you now. And wherever I am, I'll
always be your mother. I'll always love you.
More than I can ever, ever say. Be safe. Be good.

Love, Mom

Ramón was alone in his office. Outside, light snow
fell, the first of the season, and it was beautiful. It
made him so achingly lonely for Tanya he wanted to
die. He simply sat in the chair and stared out the
window and wondered how to make things right.

"Dad?" Tonio said from the doorway. In his hands
were the letters from Tanya.

Ramón swiveled, surprised. "Come on in, Tonio."

Tonio had been weeping. There was dampness still
in the extraordinarily long eyelashes. He came in and
sat on the long couch against the wall. "You should
read these."

"No. They're private, between your mom and
you."

"My mom." He moved his hand on the letters. He
took one of them out. "At least this one. It's the
oldest, the one she wrote to me the night she . . . that
my father came after her." His voice sounded stran-
gled. "At least read it."

Ramón took it. In a childish handwriting, still filled
with loops and softly formed consonants, was Antonio Quezada, and the date, almost eleven years before. He steeled himself, and opened it, unfolding a

single sheet of notebook paper, covered in the same unformed handwriting on both sides.

Dear Antonio, he read, *It's my birthday.*

When he finished, there was an ache in his chest and he had to bend his head and pinch the bridge of his nose for a long moment before he trusted himself to speak. "You've had this one a long time. I've read it before," he said at last. Having read it before didn't make it any less searing.

"I've read it, too," Tonio said. "But I didn't understand it until now." He paused. "Until Edwin and Teresa."

Ramón swallowed. "Yes."

Tonio's tears spilled over on his cheeks. "All this time, I've been so angry with her, and she did it all to keep me safe." He closed his eyes. "It's not fair what happened to her."

"No, it isn't." Ramón crossed the room and sat down next to him, and put an arm around him. "But it isn't your fault."

"You love her, don't you?"

Ramón paused. "Yes."

"Why didn't you do something to help her? Why didn't you save her?"

"I didn't know it was so bad. I didn't even know she'd divorced Victor until after all of it happened."

Tonio touched his chest. "I hate that I have his blood in me. That I'm from him."

"No." He tapped the letter they'd both read. "Do you think she would trade one minute of her life, one minute of anything that's happened, for you?"

Tonio's lip trembled, and another spill of silver tears fell on his face. Mutely, he shook his head.

"You're loved, son. So much."

"I know."

Tonio put his head against his dad's neck and wept. And Ramón just let him cry. There would be new grief, and new wonder, and even new anger before they were through, but the process, so long denied, had begun.

When the boy had calmed, Ramón said, "I want her back here. I want to marry her, but won't even ask it if you aren't ready." He sighed. "I don't want long, but I'll wait awhile if you want a little time to get used to the whole idea."

Tonio stared at him for a long time, and it was impossible for Ramón to read the expression in his eyes. "You mean we'll be a family? Mom and dad and kid?"

"Yeah. Yeah, I guess that's exactly it. Maybe even some more kids, brothers and sisters, eh?" Ramón gave him a half smile.

"I don't know about all that," he said with a frown. "But the rest is okay." He took a breath, blew it out hard. "Can I see her alone first, before you start all that?"

"Of course."

"Can we go now? I want to stop by the drug-store."

"Now is great."

They stood up. Tonio leaned forward, almost as tall as Ramón, and hugged him awkwardly. "Thank you."

"For what?"

Tonio shook his head. "For everything, I guess. For being my dad, for taking care of me when there was no one else. For stepping in."

"Hey, how could I resist?" He smiled. "You were the cutest little boy—not like now, when you're all surly teenagerness."

Tonio grinned, and the expression showed a lot of his mother. "Gee, thanks."

Ramón winked. "No problem."

From her room on the second floor of the hotel, Tanya had a view of the Sangre de Cristos, jagged against the horizon, very blue in contrast to the snow beginning to fall in thick flakes. It was chilly. She huddled closer in her sweater and got up to find another pair of socks.

She had spoken to the owner of both cafés to see if either of them needed a cook. The owners of the Blue Swan, the Mexican food place where she and Ramón had eaten the first day she came to town, were clearly suspicious that an Anglo would presume to cook Mexican, but she managed to convince them she wasn't telling lies, and they agreed to try her on weekends for a while. In the meantime, they needed a waitress for the lunch shift, starting the end of the week, and Tanya agreed to take the job.

On the way back to the hotel, she'd stopped at the bookstore and stocked up on paperback novels. It was depressing to find herself at such loose ends after all the motion of the ranch. Too much like prison.

But she refused to dwell on it. Munching M&M's from a big bag, drinking hot tea from a thermos, she tried to read an Agatha Christie mystery.

When the knock sounded, it took Tanya a moment to realize it was at her door. The visitor knocked a second time before she jumped to her feet and ran across the room, hoping against hope that Ramón had come to visit.

It was Tonio.

Stunned, Tanya simply stared at him.

"Hi," he said quietly. "Can I come in?"

"Sure. Yes." Tanya backed up, swinging the door wide to give him entrance. "Of course."

He came in and stood in the middle of the room, looking around. Awkwardly, Tanya closed the door and folded her arms over her chest. "You can sit down if you want to." She lifted her chin toward the table by the window. "Have some M&M's."

"Umm, thanks, but I really came to talk to you." He thrust an envelope into her hands. "To give this to you."

Tanya stared at him. Bright patches of color burned in his cheeks. He touched his nose, bowed his head. "Open it."

She looked down at the envelope, then turned it over and lifted the flap. Inside was a card. She took it out.

"Oh," she said in a small voice. It was a big card, fancy, with a rose frosted with white glitter that came off on her hands. In scrolly script, it read, Happy Mother's Day.

Trembling, Tanya opened it and had to blink several times to clear her vision before she could read the poem printed inside. "Roses are Red, Violets are blue, When I think of all you've done, Mother, I love you." Below that, Tonio had written, "I'm sorry I hurt your feelings. I hope we can start over fresh. Love, Antonio.

"P.S. I'm proud to be your son." '

"I had to ask the guy at the drugstore to see if he had a Mother's Day card in the back," Tonio said.

Tanya pressed her lips together, and blinked hard. She put the card down on the table blindly and put her fingers on her mouth, but the tears had been too long repressed. She looked at her son—her son—and tears ran unchecked down her face. "I didn't expect this," she whispered, fighting desperately for control.

"I read your letters," he said. "They made me cry."

Tanya shook her head. "You can't imagine...
how much I missed you," she whispered. "So much.
Every day. I've waited for you for so long." Her
breath caught and she covered her mouth and turned
away.

A little awkwardly, Tonio moved and hugged her.
"I already did all my crying. Don't be embarrassed."

Silently she hugged him, letting the tears flow down
her face, hot and free and fulsome. After a moment,
the huge wave subsided enough that she could step
back. She touched his face. "You're still you, you
know. That first day, I knew you right away in all
those kids."

He gave her his cockeyed grin. "That's what my
dad says, too." Stepping toward the door, he said,
"And speaking of him, he's here, too."

Tanya wiped her cheeks and turned around. As if
that were his cue, Ramón came into the room. "My
turn," he said.

Tonio smiled and gave them a salute. "I'll be
downstairs."

Tanya felt dizzy as Ramón moved toward her. "I
can't believe this," she whispered. "It's just...I can't
believe..."

He stopped in front of her and took her hands.
"May as well have lots of things not to believe in
then."

"What?"

He looked at her hands in his, then lifted his gaze to her face. "I wanted to let you find your own life," he said. "I had all these noble ideas about leaving you alone to be an adult without the state or some man telling you what do." He shook his head. "But there's been enough time wasted. I fell in love with you at first sight, Tanya."

"I don't want to be alone—"

"Shh, let me finish, because I might get tongue-tied if you stop me."

Tanya made a noise of disbelief. "Tongue-tied? You?"

"It could happen."

"Maybe." She chuckled. "If you were dead."

He tsked, but she saw the twinkle light his eyes. "You'll spoil this if you don't hush."

"Sorry." She bit her lip and shifted on her feet to assume a position of intent listening. A bubble of bright, pure happiness began to grow inside her.

"Where was I? Ah." His eyes sobered. "I want to marry you, Tanya. I want you to come live at the ranch with me and Tonio and all the children. I want to grow old holding you at night."

The bubble, iridescent with the promise of all the things she'd missed and wanted so much, expanded to fill her entire being. "I am so in love with you," she said softly, "that it almost seems like a dream."

"Is that a yes?"

"I want babies, Ramón. Do you want more children?"

He laughed, triumphantly and grabbed her, kissing her face. "Yes, yes, yes. A dozen, if you want. Babies everywhere." He kissed her again. "Oh, yes."

"Well, okay, then." She shrugged. "I guess I'll marry you then." She flashed an evil grin.

He laughed, and hugged her. Tanya, swept into the power of his embrace, overcome with joy, leapt on him and let him swing her around. "I can't believe I found you," she whispered into his neck. "I love you."

Ramón put her down and took her face in his hands in that gentle, cherishing gesture she so loved. "Say it again."

"I love you, Ramón."

He closed his eyes and opened them again. "And I," he said, bending to touch his lips to hers, "love you, Tanya."

Epilogue

They were married in the church at Manzanares, an old Spanish adobe that had stood there for more than two hundred years. Tonio was best man, Desmary matron of honor. Zach, dressed in a new suit, was ring bearer.

Tanya wore a simple lace dress, long and white. She'd protested for weeks that she could not wear white, that it was only for first-time brides and virgins, but Ramón had unrelentingly asked her every day to change her mind. Exasperated, she asked him why white was so important to him. "A fresh beginning," he said.

She capitulated, and standing in the warm room,

her hand on his arm, she was glad. Ramón had broken with his usual black to don a white tuxedo that made him look almost too handsome to be real.

The old bell rang out in celebration as they emerged from the church, and as if nature, too, wanted a fresh start, thick snow had begun to fall. "Beautiful," Tanya breathed.

"Yes, you are," Ramón said. He kissed her.

The reception was held in the boys' dining room, and it was as traditional as receptions came. A Spanish band played, and all the old ladies gossiped while children ran in circles in their patent leather shoes and toasts were lifted. The only nontraditional thing was the lack of alcohol served.

Teresa came in from town with her mother, a slim woman far younger than Tanya had expected, and Tonio danced with her all afternoon. "It's love," Ramón commented. "They seem so young."

"They are," Tanya said, and raised her eyes to her husband.

"Would you like to dance?" he said.

Gathering her veil and skirt, Tanya stood up. "Yes, I would. Very much."

He waited for her, and took her lightly into his embrace, and Tanya, hearing the reception laughter and music swirl all around her was suddenly transported to another wedding a long, long time ago. Remembering the youth who had kept her company, she said quietly, "We've come many miles to this day, haven't we?"

Soberly, he nodded. "Yes."

"Thank God you were there that day, Ramón. Think how our lives would be different if you weren't."

"No," he said. "I don't want to think of life without you, Tanyacita, never again."

"Thank you, Ramón. You're my knight in shining armor, you know."

"And you're my princess." With a grin, he bent and kissed her in full view of everyone. "And I'm so glad I don't have to pretend I'm not madly lusting for you every minute."

A trio of boys sent up some catcalls. "Eeeh, Mr. Quezada!"

He grinned at them. "See what you get if you behave and mind your manners? An intelligent and beautiful wife!"

Tanya laughed, and bowed, and they clapped. And then Ramón was swirling her away again and whispering what he would do with her when they were at last alone. And Tanya snuggled close, thinking of the days ahead with Tonio and Ramón, and babies and long winter nights. She sighed against him. "I'm home, at last."

"Yes," he replied against her temple. "Home at last."

* * * * *

Silhouette®

SPECIAL EDITION

COMING NEXT MONTH

#979 SUNSHINE AND THE SHADOWMASTER—
Christine Rimmer
That Special Woman!/The Jones Gang

From the moment they were thrown together, Heather Conley and
Lucas Drury were instantly drawn to each other. Giving in to that
passion made them expectant parents—but would Heather believe in
Lucas's love and stick around for the wedding?

#980 A HOME FOR ADAM—Gina Ferris Wilkins
The Family Way

Dr. Adam Stone never expected to make a house call at his own
secluded vacation cabin. But then the very pregnant Jenny Newcomb
showed on his doorstep. And one baby later, they were on their way to
an instant family!

#981 KISSES AND KIDS—Andrea Edwards
Congratulations!

Confusion over his name unexpectedly placed practical businessman
Patrick Stuart amongst Trisha Stewart and her cute kids. Pat *swore* he
was not the daddy type, but he couldn't resist sweet Trisha and her
brood for long....

#982 JOYRIDE—Patricia Coughlin
Congratulations!

Being thrown together on a cross-country drive was *not* the best way
to find a mate, Cat Bandini soon discovered. Bolton Hunter was her
complete opposite in every way—but with every passing mile, they
couldn't slow down their attraction!

#983 A DATE WITH DR. FRANKENSTEIN—Leanne Banks
Congratulations!

Andie Reynolds had spent her life taking care of others, and she'd
had it. Then sexy Eli Masters moved in next door. The neighbors
were convinced he was some sort of mad scientist. But Andie sensed
he was a single dad in need....

#984 THE AVENGER—Diana Whitney
The Blackthorn Brotherhood

Federal prosecutor Robert Arroya had time for little else but the pursuit
of justice. Then Erica Mallory and her adorable children showed him
how to trust again. But could their love survive a severe test?

MILLION DOLLAR SWEEPSTAKES (III)

No purchase necessary. To enter, follow the directions published. Method of entry may vary. For eligibility, entries must be received no later than March 31, 1996. No liability is assumed for printing errors, lost, late or misdirected entries. Odds of winning are determined by the number of eligible entries distributed and received. Prizewinners will be determined no later than June 30, 1996.

Sweepstakes open to residents of the U.S. (except Puerto Rico), Canada, Europe and Taiwan who are 18 years of age or older. All applicable laws and regulations apply. Sweepstakes offer void wherever prohibited by law. Values of all prizes are in U.S. currency. This sweepstakes is presented by Torstar Corp., its subsidiaries and affiliates, in conjunction with book, merchandise and/or product offerings. For a copy of the Official Rules send a self-addressed, stamped envelope (WA residents need not affix return postage) to: MILLION DOLLAR SWEEPSTAKES (III) Rules, P.O. Box 4573, Blair, NE 68009, USA.

EXTRA BONUS PRIZE DRAWING

No purchase necessary. The Extra Bonus Prize will be awarded in a random drawing to be conducted no later than 5/30/96 from among all entries received. To qualify, entries must be received by 3/31/96 and comply with published directions. Drawing open to residents of the U.S. (except Puerto Rico), Canada, Europe and Taiwan who are 18 years of age or older. All applicable laws and regulations apply; offer void wherever prohibited by law. Odds of winning are dependent upon number of eligibile entries received. Prize is valued in U.S. currency. The offer is presented by Torstar Corp., its subsidiaries and affiliates in conjunction with book, merchandise and/or product offering. For a copy of the Official Rules governing this sweepstakes, send a self-addressed, stamped envelope (WA residents need not affix return postage) to: Extra Bonus Prize Drawing Rules, P.O. Box 4590, Blair, NE 68009, USA.

SWP-S895

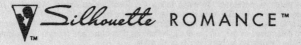

Silhouette ROMANCE™

Silhouette Romance presents the latest of Diana Palmer's much-loved series

Long Tall Texans

COLTRAIN'S PROPOSAL
DIANA PALMER

Louise Blakely was about to leave town when Jebediah Coltrain made a startling proposal—a fake engagement to save his reputation! But soon Louise suspected that the handsome doctor had more on his mind than his image. Could Jeb want Louise for life?

Coming in September from Silhouette Romance. Look for this book in our "Make-Believe Marriage" promotion.

DPLTT

As a Privileged Woman,
you'll be entitled to all these *Free Benefits.* And *Free Gifts,* too.

To thank you for buying our books, we've designed an exclusive FREE program called *PAGES & PRIVILEGES™.* You can enroll with just one Proof of Purchase, and get the kind of luxuries that, until now, you could only read about.

*B*IG HOTEL DISCOUNTS

A privileged woman stays in the finest hotels. And so can you—at up to 60% off! Imagine standing in a hotel check-in line and watching as the guest in front of you pays $150 for the same room that's only costing you $60. Your *Pages & Privileges* discounts are good at Sheraton, Marriott, Best Western, Hyatt and thousands of other fine hotels all over the U.S., Canada and Europe.

*F*REE DISCOUNT TRAVEL SERVICE

A privileged woman is always jetting to romantic places. When <u>you</u> fly, just make one phone call for the lowest published airfare at time of booking—<u>or double the difference back!</u> PLUS—

you'll get a $25 voucher to use the first time you book a flight AND <u>5% cash back on every ticket you buy thereafter through the travel service!</u>

$\mathcal{F}$REE GIFTS!

A privileged woman is always getting wonderful gifts.
Luxuriate in rich fragrances that will stir your senses (and his). This gift-boxed assortment of fine perfumes includes three popular scents, each in a beautiful designer bottle. <u>Truly Lace</u>...This luxurious fragrance unveils your sensuous side. <u>L'Effleur</u>...discover the romance of the Victorian era with this soft floral. <u>Muguet des bois</u>...a single note floral of singular beauty.

YOURS FREE!

$50 VALUE

$\mathcal{F}$REE INSIDER TIPS LETTER

A privileged woman is always informed. And you'll be, too, with our free letter full of fascinating information and sneak previews of upcoming books.

$\mathcal{M}$ORE GREAT GIFTS & BENEFITS TO COME

A privileged woman always has a lot to look forward to. And so will you. You get all these wonderful FREE gifts and benefits now with only one purchase...and there are no additional purchases required. However, each additional retail purchase of Harlequin and Silhouette books brings you a step closer to even more great FREE benefits like half-price movie tickets... and even more FREE gifts.

L'Effleur...This basketful of romance lets you discover L'Effleur from head to toe, heart to home.

Truly Lace... A basket spun with the sensuous luxuries of Truly Lace, including Dusting Powder in a reusable satin and lace covered box.

Complete the Enrollment Form in the front of this book and mail it with this Proof of Purchase.

PROOF OF PURCHASE
Offer expires October 31, 1996

SSE-PP4